Mark g   ɪk.
"Are you f   A
lopsided griɪ. ᴏᴘ.ᴇᴀᴜ ᴀᴄ.ᴏᴏᴏ ɪɪɪs ɪace like the Cheshire Cat's smile in *Alice in Wonderland.*

"Of course not." Nikki felt herself flushing at her moment of weakness in saying what she did. The trajectory of their footsteps going back and forth from the counter brought them face to face with each other, forcing her to look up straight into his eyes and seeing an amused look there.

"I was just asking if the cooking was alright," she said, feeling deflated. Darned if she was angling for a compliment from this unimaginative man who probably couldn't compliment his way out of a circle of leprechauns. He stood in front of her like a basketball player blocking a pass, except his arms weren't raised. He took the dishes from her and placed them on the counter.

"The cooking is fine. And here's a reward for the chef." He tipped her chin up slowly and placed a kiss full on her lips. Slipping his arm around her waist, his mouth brushed hers again, this time more demanding.

Nikki brought the palms of her hands against his chest to push him away, feeling his corded muscles beneath her palms. Then, swept away by the musky scent of his aftershave and his firm grasp, she could resist no longer. Her arms entwined around his neck and she returned his urgent kiss with a matching fervor of her own.

Minutes became an eternity, silent but for the drumbeat of her heart, or was it the thud of his? She couldn't tell. Enough of this arrant lack of control on her part—whatever he had in mind she didn't have to follow along with him for the ride. Why did she have to fall all to pieces at his firm touch? Nikki struggled out of his arms at last.

ട്ട   ଏ

Rekha Ambardar

Maid to Order

Echelon Press

Echelon Press
56 Sawyer Circle #354
Memphis, TN 38103

Copyright © 2005 by R. Ambardar
ISBN: 1-59080-216-0
www.echelonpress.com

First Echelon Press paperback printing: May 2005

Cover Art © Nathalie Moore
2005 Arianna Best In category Award
Editor: Elizabeth Baird

Printed in Lavergne, TN, USA

Also by Rekha Ambardar

His Harbor Girl
(Whiskey Creek Press)

Dedication

For my parents, who believed I could.

CHAPTER ONE

Mark Runyon sprinted up the steps of the modernized brownstone in Chicago's Jefferson Park and pulled open the grill-reinforced door. He stepped inside and grinned at Jack Delaney, the supervisor, through the long glass window of his office in Tivoli Terrace Apartments.

He glanced at the elevator briefly and shook his head. No, not the easy way up today. He'd been in meetings all day the last few days, and had had no time for his usual tennis game. Better take the stairs. He could handle four flights, no problem.

He loosened his tie and started climbing. In his briefcase, he carried the graphical representations of the new senior citizens' condominium he wanted to look over. David Roth, an associate, had commended Mark on the new advertising slant for REA Inc.–"You'll Know You're Home." The words sang in his mind like a jingle. It reminded him of the company's mission statement of putting the client first. This new project was his baby and he had had a special person in mind when he developed this idea.

Mark caught his breath as he remembered something. He hadn't been able to make the Children's Heart Foundation fundraiser the other evening, and now he'd never hear the end of it from Gran. Dear, lovable Gran. What was it she'd mentioned? That she had found a new housekeeper to replace

1

dragon lady, Mrs. Babbitt.   Good, he could stop ordering Chinese takeout from now on.

Footsteps slowing, Mark climbed on.   He reached the fourth floor, unlocked the door, and walked into a large apartment bathed in the late afternoon sun.   He stashed his briefcase on the side table in the hall and pulled off the tie that felt like a choke chain better used in dog obedience classes.

Suddenly, something appeared strangely wrong.   Things were in place all right–the expensive oil paintings in their silver-bracketed frames in the hall, and the living room billowing out at the far end with its soft chamois leather upholstery furniture.   The vases were filled with flowers, Mark's standing request to the cleaning temp.

Then why did he feel like the three bears walking in on Goldilocks?   At the end of the hall, he spied two suitcases partly hidden by the wall, and a sneaker tumbled against it nearby.   Alert to the last nerve, he followed the signs as a nature lover might follow markings in the woods.

On the sprawling living room sofa, a small, blonde, tousle-haired waif lay curled with an arm resting on a rounded cheek, her sneaker-clad foot dangling over the edge of the sofa.   Her blue jeans were molded over eye-catching curves as she lay fast asleep, breathing evenly.

Mark stood there, his tie draped around his neck, a hand on one hip, and watched her for a few moments.   A frown formed on his forehead and then slowly disappeared.   Curled on the sofa in that childlike way, she looked pretty.   Thick sooty lashes lay like veils over her eyes, and the white long-sleeved shirt with its sleeves rolled up gave her a tomboyish air that was curiously attractive.

Mark pulled himself together.   He had no business standing here getting an eyeful of Sleeping Beauty.   But who was she and how did she get in?

The girl stirred and opened her eyes. Green, he noticed, sea green. Mark cleared his throat. "Miss, I think you're in the wrong place."

"What? Oh...I..." She sat up, her hand going to her head. "Ouch! This is Tivoli Terrace Apartments, isn't it? Ellen Carstens sent me. I'm Nikki Slater, the new housekeeper."

Mark slowly pulled the dangling tie off his neck and crumpled it in his hand. Had Gran lost her mind? Was this another one of the charity cases she forever championed? Did she really think this elf-like girl could handle the work of Mrs. Babbitt? Mrs. Babbitt even scared dust away, and when she left, she had brought in a temp just like herself–frontline combat material, the original drill sergeant. He unbuttoned his collar. "How did you get in?" This ought to be good, he thought.

"The super let me in. I have a note from Ellen." She fumbled in her jeans pocket for a while, wriggling every which way.

Mark looked away, very conscious of the girl's allure, the hair around her face in curly wisps, the perfect mouth.

"Here it is," she said finally, fishing out a crumpled piece of paper. "It's addressed to you, so the super agreed to let me in."

Mark took the note from her. "Dear Mark," it said. "I'm sending Nikki as promised. She's a good worker and will be a help to you. She needs a place to stay. Perhaps she could use the spare apartment adjoining yours? Take care of yourself and try not to work too hard. Love, Gran."

Mark allowed himself a half-chuckle, recognizing his grandmother's concern for him. How like her to spring a surprise like this on him! The girl looked as if she had packed her life's belongings into two suitcases. She probably needed the money badly and Ellen stepped in to help. Fine with him, he could go along with a gag to humor his grandmother.

The extent of the situation dawned on Mark like a neon light gaining power by the second. The girl sat groggily on the sofa and pushed the hair away from her eyes. It suddenly hit him that she was to stay in his spare apartment. Mark swallowed hard on that one. Too bad she couldn't leave at the end of the day as Mrs. Babbitt had done. Someone like her was too much to handle when the new construction project was just getting underway. He didn't want a distracting female hovering next door.

Mark raked his fingers through his hair. "If you can cook and keep the apartment clean, it's fine with me. The apartment you will use has a separate entrance. In fact," he said, going to a narrow closet and pulling out a key that hung on the inside of the door, "I'll show you around." He glanced at her suitcases. "You might want to bring those."

Nikki got up. Small built, she barely reached his shoulder. What was Gran thinking when she sent this puny little urchin his way? He hoped like heck she could do some work, though he doubted if she was much good. Mild irritation assaulted him as he led the way to the other apartment. He opened the door and stood aside to let her enter. "This door is left unlocked," he said.

They stood in the foyer flooded with the light of the setting sun. Mark watched with amusement as Nikki walked over to the window and stared at the scenery outside. He had to admit it looked nice this time of year when leaves were starting to come in the trees.

"It's beautiful," she said, coming away from the window. Her gaze fell on a glass and steel abstract structure on the black marble-topped table in the foyer.

"Like it?" he asked.

Nikki nodded. "But what is it?"

"It's a miniature skyscraper. It's in there somewhere, if you look hard enough." Mark laughed. "What's the matter?"

The dimpled smile that had looked promising turned into a puzzled expression. "What do you do?" Her eyes opened wide and a sharpness laced her tone.

"Construct buildings."

"You work for the Runyon Corporation?"

"My father and I own it. I'm Mark Runyon. We also have a battalion of relatives working for us. You sure you're okay? You look ill." Mark lurched forward suddenly and caught her by the arm to steady her. "Whoa."

What *was* the matter with her? This was an odd time to be groggy. Was she one of those party animals in a perpetual state of hangover? Or maybe she was just hungry, which was probably why Gran got involved. The girl was probably too poor to afford a square meal a day.

"Are you hungry? I was going to order Chinese food." He was, after all, a volunteer for Big Brothers, he could help one more down-and-out person, except he had to admit she didn't make him feel like any brother. Not with her curves and those come-hither bedroom eyes.

"No, no. I'm fine." She appeared to gain control of herself.

"Well, let me show you the apartment. Then you can settle in. Is this all the luggage you have?"

"For now. I sold my furniture since this place came furnished."

"Of course." Mark hoped he sounded convincing in accepting her words at face value.

He helped her carry the suitcases and crossed an archway leading to a suite of rooms: a living room, bedroom, and kitchen.

"This is it. Think you can manage here?" He hardly expected her to balk–it was furnished in a neat, elegant style. "When you're ready, you can come over to my apartment. I'd like to go over a few things with you."

He strode out leaving her standing in the hallway, suitcases standing on either side of her like two short, protective pillars. Did Gran have any idea what she'd gotten him into? Foisting on him a young woman with a propensity for taking naps in strange surroundings?

Nikki threw her suitcase on the bed and looked around the room. From finding out her apartment building was turning condo to landing here in this snazzy apartment was as good as being whacked on the head with a baseball bat and then dumped into ice-cold water. On the one hand, gratitude welled up inside her and she thought of Ellen's promise to find her a job and an apartment. On the other hand, realizing that Mark was *the* Runyon who came from the long line of architects whose praises her mother had sung, was the biggest surprise yet. It had taken all her willpower to pull herself together when he mentioned his work.

Her glance swept toward a door leading to the balcony with ornate wrought iron railings creating a quaint, European air. The expression "compact yet stylish" took on new meaning. Whoever undertook the decor of this suite had classic good taste in the colors and fabrics. The floor tiles were white, so cool that Nikki decided to walk barefoot. It felt like wading in clear, shallow water. Remembering the soft beige upholstery of the living room furniture, Nikki decided that flowers would add a blaze of color.

Which was all well and good. Luxury was not exactly unknown to her, but what was she doing in Mark Runyon's orbit? She'd struck out on her own to get away from the umbrella of family name and money to prove her own mettle, only to fall right into the midst of the family her mother had wanted Nikki to marry into. Still, this guy seemed almost tolerable. It could be an act, of course. The men she'd known had been either wolves in sheep's clothing, octopuses, or just plain greedy for money. Which category did Mark Runyon belong to? Tread carefully here, girl, she said to herself.

As Nikki clicked open the suitcases and started emptying one of them onto the bed, her mind wandered to her plans as her hands got busy. She had less than a year to finish catering school and needed the money; how fortunate that Ellen had negotiated a good salary, and Nikki didn't have to pay rent. Surely, she could swallow her dislike for the entitlement that wealthy folks seemed to have and follow her own dream?

A few minutes later, one suitcase was emptied and its contents hung in the closet. The other one could wait, she'd better meet Mark properly and discuss her duties. She moved toward the large dresser mirror and studied herself. She looked a fright!

Over the weekend, Nikki had reduced her belongings to two suitcases and saw no reason to delay her move. Today, she was tired. It had been a hectic day and she came to Mark's apartment directly after class. The last thing she expected to do was zonk out on the comfortable sofa in Mark's apartment. Her hand flew up to her hair. It looked as if it had been whipped up with an eggbeater, her shirt hung out of her jeans, and she needed a wash.

She headed to the bathroom and briskly splashed water on

her face. Now she began to feel sane, or awake anyway. Eyes still closed, she clutched at a towel and wiped her face.

Better, she thought. She approached the door of the adjoining apartment and knocked. Getting no response, she opened the door and let herself in.

Nikki blinked and looked around, breathless with curiosity. Earlier, she hadn't taken the opportunity to really study her surroundings, but now twilight had fallen and the faint remnants of a pink haze still lingered outside. Crystal chandeliers lit up the spacious living room to a dazzling white. Black and white floor tiles were arranged in an interesting design, and on the wall hung a good-sized pewter clock shaped like the sun with irregular-shaped rays radiating from it. A work of art.

"Mr. Runyon?" Nikki called. Formality would keep things between them in proper perspective.

"In here," a voice called out from a room off to the side. The study? She moved in that direction.

Mark sat in front of a laptop computer in a room lined with shelves holding thick books, while near the window stood a big drafting table with a lamp bent directly over it. A thick blue sheet spread across the table and held down with paperweights caught her attention.

He got up. "Are you settled in? How do you like your apartment?" he asked.

"Pretty much, and yes, the apartment is just fine," Nikki replied, telling herself mentally to stop gawking at him. Fate must have it in for her–Nikki couldn't think of any other reason why it would throw her into the path of this knock-out guy. It wasn't fair.

Earlier, even in a sleepy haze, she'd noticed he was very easy on the eye. Now he leaned against the computer table, his gaze flicking over her in a deliberate appraisal. Tall and broad-shouldered, his jeans followed narrow hips, muscular thighs, and long, sturdy legs with precision. The dark blue shirt with sleeves rolled to the elbows revealed tanned forearms folded casually across the chest. For somebody who apparently worked as hard as he did, he sported an incredible tan, glowing and golden brown.

Handsome, she thought, trying to appear unimpressed. Melting brown eyes with laugh lines at the corners arrested her attention and thick chestnut brown hair sprang back from a broad forehead. Early-to-mid-thirties, she guessed.

A faint smile of amusement curved the corners of his mouth. He'd noticed her staring. "Miss, er…" He straightened and extended his hand, encasing hers with ease and poise.

"Please call me Nikki," she said, a little unsettled by the firm grip. His hands were strong with well-shaped fingers.

"Then you'll have to call me Mark," he said with a grin. "Now, let's go into the living room and discuss your duties. Enough with the design software." He grimaced at the computer screen and strode out of the study.

Nikki made it a point to sit bolt upright in one of the more uncomfortable-looking chairs in the living room. Being found fast asleep on the sofa still rankled, and she vowed never to be caught like that again.

"How did you meet my grandmother?" he asked. He sat on the sofa, an arm extended along the back of it.

"We're taking cooking classes together at the Saunders Institute. I needed a place to stay after being told by the manager that our building was going to get a complete overhaul. Too bad, because the Nob Hill Apartments were close to the Institute."

Mark removed his resting arm, visibly jolted. "Nob Hill Apartments? You were a resident there?"

Nikki looked up. "Yes, why?"

"Because I know the place. In fact, I own it," he said.

Suddenly the truth hit her like a lightening bolt. The manager had mentioned somebody who owned other buildings as well, and was an architect in the Runyon Corporation. But there were so many Runyons that it could have been anyone. At the time, she'd been too preoccupied to make the connection. Nikki felt herself flush with anger at being the recipient of his high-handed deal-making. "Do you realize what you've done?"

"Now, look," Mark said, his voice controlled compared to Nikki's, which had risen an octave higher. "We're assisting the residents in finding apartments—at least, those that want our help." He paused for a moment. "You, obviously, didn't need it because my grandmother was helping you."

Nikki bristled at the cavalier way in which he spoke. "Ellen was good enough to come to my aid," she replied. "Otherwise, I'd have been out of a place to stay. And I needed to be near the Saunders Institute."

She probably sounded hysterical, but it was the same uncaring reaction she'd grown up with, when her parents expected hired help to take care of her while they went on endless travels abroad. The human element didn't seem to matter to them. Images floated in her mind's eye—band concerts and brownie meetings missed because Daddy had business trips and Mother had society functions to attend. The one who taught her about feelings and caring had been her young nanny, Celia. And about baking cookies and cakes, which had produced Nikki's love of cooking.

This gem of physical perfection sitting in front of her had

those same expectations as her parents times ten, Nikki thought, unclenching her sweaty hands. How else did he think he could find residences for the people who had been displaced when the building came down?

"It's just like my grandmother to take some needy person under her wing and look out for them," Mark said. "I wouldn't want to see her hurt."

"Don't worry," Nikki replied. "My intentions are honorable." Irritation welled up at the insinuation that she might be, in some way, taking advantage of Ellen's trusting nature because she was poor. Was he guilty of snobbery, too? Never mind, she'd give him a piece of her mind if the situation arose.

"Ellen has been taken advantage of in the past," Mark said.

"I understand your concern," Nikki replied. "But she is a good friend and we have mutual respect for each other." Nikki tucked her hair behind her ear. "Now," she said briskly, "Tell me what you need done, and we can go from there."

"Right." Mark stood up. "As you can see, this is a large apartment. It will have to be kept clean and dusted. Mrs. Babbitt did both the cooking and cleaning. After she left, I've been eating out and getting a temp in to clean. Can you manage the cleaning as well?"

Nikki could tell he liked a spotless environment. His study had the look of a fastidious executive. "Of course. But since I'm taking cooking classes, I'll need time off."

A twinkle glistened in his eyes. "You're one of those gourmet cooks?"

"I've had an interest in cooking ever since I can remember. Cooking is a work of art," Nikki said, momentarily being transported to the world of the culinary masterpieces she hoped to soon produce. "Few people realize how involved it can be."

Mark listened without speaking. Nikki felt his dark, luminous eyes sizing her up. She couldn't shake off the feeling that he wasn't really taking her at her word, and that it had to do with his grandmother.

Nikki chuckled inwardly. Ellen was the best friend she had. Let him writhe with suspicion. *Serves him right!*

"Take the time you need for your classes, just as long as the work is done around here." And he meant it, she could tell. It reminded Nikki of her Dad giving orders to their driver and the riding instructor who came once a week. He was brilliant in the world of business, but he was pushy in handling people.

Now, Nikki had half a mind to put on a downstairs-maid act and say, "Yes, sir. Right away, sir," and bob a curtsy as they did on the PBS shows she sometimes watched.

"Where do you keep the cleaning supplies?" Nikki asked.

"Right over there." Mark nodded in the direction of a wide hall closet. "There's a washer and dryer in the back room. You're welcome to use them for your own wash. Most of my clothes go to the cleaners, but I prefer to do my everyday clothes myself, those I wash here."

Nikki nodded, slowly getting a picture of the kind of man he must be—no nonsense, and keeps to himself.

"Oh, and you'll need to keep the refrigerator stocked. I'll leave a list on the table."

"What time will you need breakfast?"

"Eight. I'll let you know if I have to leave earlier for a breakfast meeting with clients from out of town," Mark said. "I have only a light breakfast of toast, orange juice, and coffee. And a boiled egg now and then."

Nikki watched him thoughtfully. Being the busy executive, he probably skipped lunch. No wonder Ellen worried about him. Though tall and muscular, he was still her baby.

"Dinner's the only meal I really eat," he said.

"Figures."

"I beg your pardon?"

"Your grandmother hinted that you were a workaholic."

Mark grinned. "I just like what I do."

The phone jingled somewhere. Wondering where it was hidden, Nikki looked behind her and saw a cell phone on a black glass-topped table near an ornate walnut screen.

Mark picked it up. "Hello? Well, how are you? What time is it over there?" He paced the room as he talked, his face beaming with animation.

Obviously somebody he likes, Nikki thought. A client?

"Good. I'm glad it's going well. As one of the investors in the shopping center, you have a say in its design. Glad the others are pleased with the layout. By the way, thanks for the clock and the screen. They are both in the living room. G'bye." He clicked a button and clapped the phone shut.

Mark turned to her. "From Kuala Lumpur. Four investors are financing a huge shopping mall with an ancient Egyptian theme, believe it or not. A bit extravagant for my tastes, but to each his own, I suppose."

"Do you have many business deals overseas?" Nikki tried to sound politely casual.

"Far East and the Middle East. My father did an urban planning project in Dahram." He picked up the phone again. "I was going to call for some Chinese takeout. Would you like to join me?"

Nikki got up. "No, I have to finish unpacking. Tomorrow, I have an early start after doing the housework." But she had to call Ellen before that.

"Help yourself to a sandwich from the fridge," Mark said.

"Thanks." She'd have to do some grocery shopping and stock her own refrigerator. She wondered how it would all work out, and if she'd done the right thing moving next door to a rich, drop-dead gorgeous guy. It would have been a lot easier if he'd been just an average everyday employer instead of somebody who seemed to unsettle her with his lucid amber eyes.

Nikki shook herself of the handful of potent, male personality she had just left in the other apartment, entered the foyer of her apartment, and looked for the phone. It sat in the living room, a lime green, corded number.

Nikki picked up the receiver, punched the buttons, and waited.

"Hello? Ellen?"

A clear, low voice came over the line. "Nikki? Are you settled in, dear?"

"Yes, thanks." Nikki chuckled at the way Ellen came to the point efficiently. So characteristic of her. "And thank you for keeping my family background a secret."

"You're welcome. If you didn't want to make it known you were in any way connected with the banking family, that's your business. If anything, it's to your credit you're paying your way through school. Meantime, I'm getting something out of it, too."

"What?"

"My grandson gets wholesome, home-cooked meals and someone to keep an eye on him."

Nikki smiled to herself at Ellen's innocent choice of words and, saying goodbye to her friend, hung up.

Mark had been conscious of his gaze following Nikki as

she left for her apartment. He put his thoughts on hold for a while and dialed the number of Shanghai Delight.

"Carry-out for Runyon. Chop suey and sesame chicken, please. You know where to bring it." He hung up. The restaurant owners knew him like a member of their family, and anybody coming in would be cleared by the security system. The doorman would buzz upstairs and let him know.

He felt a slight disappointment that Nikki had declined to join him, and he hardly knew why. Perhaps because she showed spirit and independence. Had to have, if she was putting herself through catering school and planning to set up business. She probably had visions of making money in her venture, never having had any. He knew the value of money, so he couldn't exactly fault her for it.

He shook his head. Those pool-green eyes seemed to pierce his soul for some reason. Yet, there was something about her that he couldn't quite fathom. Was it grasping ambition? Of course. Somebody as poor as she was would want to vault herself out of her present situation. What kind of family did she come from? And was she really here to work, or to earn some quick money in a "cushy" job? Well, he'd just see to it that she earned her salary.

CHAPTER TWO

Mark buttered his toast and laid it on the plate. "I expect my grandmother to take up sky diving or mountain climbing with a sherpa in tow any day."

"You mean she's not afraid to try anything new?" Nikki wiped down the kitchen counter until it shone.

"That, and she doesn't like being bored," Mark bit into his toast.

"Good for her. She's doing very well in cooking classes." She remembered Ellen's delectable entree creations, soups, and desserts. Nikki followed, a close second in cooking demonstrations and competitions. "Consider yourself lucky she's your grandmother."

"This egg's runny," Mark stared at his plate.

"It's been boiled for three minutes." Puzzled, Nikki went over to inspect it. Not runny, she thought, just soft.

"Mrs. Babbitt's eggs were rock solid. I like them that way." There was no petulance in his voice, just a bald statement of fact as if he had the final say in the matter and couldn't be budged.

"Okay. Duly noted." Nikki felt her nostrils quiver with irritation.

No point in quibbling about a boiled egg. She needed this job not just for the money, but for the cooking experience–it would provide a solid background for starting her business later.

"If you don't need anything else, I'll be off to the Institute and back later to do the cleaning."

Nikki had been up early and now yearned for a cool, refreshing shower. She glanced at Mark and envied his fresh appearance. Hair slightly damp from his shower, he adjusted the sleeve of his tan suit. Nikki clenched her fist over the kitchen towel. She didn't want to feel this awareness of Mark; he was only her employer and nothing more.

"Fine. I'll be late coming home. I've left the housekeeping money and a list on the table. Let me know if you need anything else." Mark got up from the table and reached for his briefcase.

"Do you want dinner ready?" Nikki asked.

"Yes, something light. Don't know how things will go today at the office, I have several meetings with clients. I'll see you later. Have a nice day." He strode out the front door.

Nikki stood staring after him and chewed on her lower lip. So this would be the pattern, day after day. She'd see Mark for a while in the morning and when he came home from work. Short as that time was, her temples pounded at the thought and it put a scare into her. Would she be able to concentrate on her side of the bargain with his aftershave cologne sabotaging her hardheaded resolve, and the occasional lopsided grin flashing at her like a sudden beam of light from nowhere?

Showered and dressed, Nikki took the elevator to the sub-basement and walked out, the doors closing behind her. As an employee and resident of the building, Mark had found Nikki a spot to park her unobtrusive gray Ford sedan.

She drove out into the bright sunshine, which promised a pleasant, achievement-filled day. Lowering the window just a little, Nikki let the fresh air sift in and pat her on the face as she eased onto the expressway.

After twenty minutes, the Saunders Institute slid into view. It was a fairly new, whitewashed building standing by itself in a square lot surrounded by a concrete enclosure.

She squinted as sunlight reflected off the black-glass exterior of the Institute. Automobiles whizzing by on the expressway kept up a constant drone in the background as she parked in the car-lined lot.

Nikki ran up the steps, through the wide doors, and into the main lobby which was decorated with display cases containing cooking trophies awarded to instructors and graduates. Gloria Kettering, Director of the Institute, made it a point to have at least one speaker a week hold a demonstration class on entrees, souffles, pastry techniques, or brown sauces. She took the wide staircase to the second floor and proceeded to the Fairview Room, a large room with state-of-the-art conveniences–a convection oven, a large microwave oven, two cooking ranges, an island in the center with a wood-top counter for chopping, and two refrigerators. Shiny copper-bottomed utensils hung from hooks on the wall.

A knot of students walked in chatting as they put on aprons and tucked their hair into nets. Nikki fished out an apron and hairnet from a large shoulder bag and put them on. Female chatter grew to a crescendo as the only three male students in the class stood by quietly, appearing left out of the energetic group.

Today's cooking topic was Creole Flounder. Signey Henderson, a senior instructor, would do a partial demo, after which the students were scheduled to work on their own, two people to a dish.

Nikki glanced around for Ellen, but didn't see her. She

wanted to chat with her after class to let her know how things were going.

The room started filling up and Signey walked in carrying a plastic supermarket bag.

"Hello, all." She emptied the bag. "I have the ingredients laid out here on the counter. The flounder is thawed, so we can start right away." She looked around. "Everyone here?"

"Ellen isn't here yet," Nikki said, concern gnawing at her stomach. Would Ellen miss the demo? Nikki had counted on seeing her today. Maybe she could also fill in some blanks about Mark.

"She is now." Ellen walked in, apron in hand.

Nikki smiled at her. "You made it."

"Traffic was terrible today. Bennett arrived bright and early, so it wasn't his fault," Ellen said. Like Greyhound passengers, the older woman left the driving to her trusted driver. Ellen gave Nikki a scrutinizing look and took her elbow. "How is your job working out?"

Nikki glanced at Signey before replying. Their instructor was bustling around setting up for the demonstration.

"Quite well. And I like the apartment," Nikki said in a whisper. About Mark she wasn't quite sure–he managed to send her heart into thudding acrobatics whenever she saw him. These feelings were not what a housekeeper was supposed to have for her employer.

"Come on, Nikki. You can tell me." A look of anxiety flitted across Ellen's fine features. "You don't like your job? Mark?"

"No, no." Nikki still kept her voice low. "Actually, the job's easy." She felt a surge of warmth toward Ellen, an alien experience since her own mother never showed her any concern or affection. Ellen obviously cared enough to be worried about her.

"Then it's Mark," Ellen said quietly without taking her gaze off Nikki's face.

"Mark's a good employer." Nikki was careful to avoid any inflection in her voice. She just never expected him to be a heart-stopper, which presented a problem.

"Then what is it?"

"I wanted to explain why I didn't want Mark to know I'm the daughter of the Slater who owns Midwest Savings Bank. I took the job to pay my tuition, and there's no need for him to know all my personal problems."

Nikki hoped Ellen would understand. She wasn't being secretive, it just seemed unnecessary for Mark to know her motive for working as a housekeeper. Wealthy as he was, he surely wouldn't see what it meant to her. Besides, if a prospective employer knew she was rich, it wouldn't speak much for her capacity for domestic work.

"Flounder has the least amount of fat," Signey was saying, jolting Nikki's attention to the front of the room. Nikki and Ellen approached the counter and watched Signey place filets into a greased oblong baking dish.

Nikki made a mental note to chat with Signey after class. The instructor advised her on the catering business she would one day open, and Nikki found these suggestions invaluable. She knew the instructor would be able to refer clientele to her, and she needed the input. Signey had been trained at the Cordon Bleu in London and was a member of the International Association of Culinary Professionals.

Nikki and Ellen worked with Signey, mixing all the ingredients: chopped green pepper, tomatoes, lemon juice, and coarsely ground pepper. Minutes later, after taking the dish out of the oven, they garnished it with green pepper rings and tomato wedges. Nikki sniffed the tangy aroma appreciatively. There was something about cooking that gave her a sense of creation unlike any other she'd experienced.

After class, Nikki and Ellen went into the lounge and helped themselves to coffee. "My feet are killing me," Ellen said. "It feels so good to sit down and sip coffee."

The lounge faced a clump of trees behind the building. Except for two people reading and the custodian emptying trash, it was quiet.

"I have a confession," Ellen said between sips. "You're helping me by working for Mark."

Nikki laughed. "How's that?"

"Your home-cooked meals will make him want to settle down."

"He's a grown man, Ellen. Nobody can make him do anything," Nikki teased her.

"I know, dear. But he doesn't seem to know what's good for him, working overtime and dating women who probably don't know how to cook. Something tells me you'll be a good influence for him."

"Don't expect too much from me. I'm only doing my job."

"And I have every confidence in you." Ellen got up and gathered her voluminous tote bag. "See you tomorrow, dear." She waved exuberantly at Nikki and bustled out of the room.

Nikki held the keys between her teeth and put the bag of groceries down. She unlocked Mark's apartment door and dragged in her own grocery bag, then leaned back against the door to shut it.

She emptied the contents of one bag into the refrigerator and made sure things were arranged where he could see them—milk, eggs, and sandwich meat in the special compartment off to the side.

Nikki placed a package of chicken in the sink and glanced at her watch. Four o'clock. She'd have to start dinner soon. A casserole, she thought, something that would cook while she cleaned the apartment.

She took a quick tour of the place to find out where things were kept. Plastic containers with potatoes were in the cabinet under the sink; the cabinets above had carousels with condiments, spices, and dried herbs neatly arranged and labeled. The cutlery was stored in drawers along the black marble counter that extended around the room.

Nikki moved into the dining area. Expensive dinnerware, crystal decanters, and wine glasses displayed on a glass-and-bleached-wood shelf with mirrored backing caught her eye. The space was shared by a dining table that could easily seat twelve.

She remembered that Mark had mentioned the hall closet. She opened it and found cleaning items stored there–mop, bucket, vacuum cleaner, spray cleanser, floor polish, and cloth dusters. A blue apron hung on a peg. She drew in a breath; everything she needed to keep the apartment spotless was right under her nose. She wouldn't have to buy anything.

Nikki looked around, running her hand over tabletops, shelves, and stone ornaments. No telltale signs of dust; the temp had obviously been doing a competent job and she would have to match that. First, she had to put away her own groceries.

Groceries stored in her refrigerator, Nikki returned to Mark's apartment to start dinner. She opened the package of chicken, skinned, and cleaned it, and placed it in a casserole dish she found in the oven compartment. She took out cans of mushroom soup and tomatoes and poured them over the chicken. Something simple today, Mark had said. Chicken casserole, baby carrots, baked potatoes, and rolls. One day he'd thank her for this healthy fare.

Satisfied with a task accomplished, she placed the chicken and potatoes in the oven, briskly wiped her hands on her apron, then set to work on the housecleaning.

An hour later, feeling hot, sweaty, and irritable, she drew the back of her hand across her face and flapped the collar of her shirt. Who said a housekeeper's job was easy? Anyone?

She leaned on the long-handled mop trying to remember the cheery television commercials about floor and lemon-scented furniture polish from which stars sprang out in sickening profusion. She unknowingly clutched a handful of hair and then, realizing what she was doing, shook her head. She'd thought this was going to be a breeze when the most she'd done was run a vacuum across the floor of her apartment. Fortunately, the temp had done her job well; all Nikki had to do was tidy the rooms and not let dust accumulate.

With the duster tucked into her jeans waistband, she went looking for the bedroom. It was large and airy, with a king-sized bed in the center. Four large pillows were propped up against the headboard, bearing the imprint of its occupant as if he had spent the whole night reading and had dozed off over the material. Nikki could imagine Mark reading, his chest bare against the dark maroon sheets. Her face heated at the thought. What was coming over her?

Nikki stood back for a moment, curiosity overcoming her as she took in the dresser with wood-backed hair brushes and a shiny metal tray holding loose change, jeans and T-shirts tossed over a large antique chest at the foot of the bed.

Her gaze scanned every detail as she stood there holding the caddy of cleaning agents in hand. Why did the room interest her so? Because it gave an inkling of the man she worked for? For a wealthy, spoiled guy, the room was surprisingly free of frills—it contained just the everyday things he used. Her eyes narrowed as she looked around the room that spoke of single male habits—the monogrammed green robe tossed on the floor, papers with numbers on them sticking out of manila envelopes...had he forgotten to take them with him this morning?

Setting down the cleanser caddy, she picked up clothes and folded them. The scent from his cologne still hung in the air and she stopped a moment to savor its brisk, spicy fragrance.

Nikki folded, dusted, stacked, sorted, and sprayed, and when she was finished cleaning, the bedroom and attached bathroom smelled fresh and clean. She would swear she could see stars bursting through the shiny surfaces.

Nikki was going full speed ahead now. She seemed to have suddenly unlocked the secret to good housekeeping—concentration and the will to do a good job.

Later, as she put the mop, duster, and cleansers back into the closet and admired the results of her toil, the sunburst clock showed close to six o'clock. She'd have to hurry with preparing the baby carrots. Was she expected to wait table with a white napkin draped over her arm? She was not sure how she should act, never having been a maid before. Confusion and pride jostled for first position in her feelings just now—she was just earning her way; playacting wasn't part of her job description. Was it?

For somebody who'd always had her room cleaned and her way cleared of tiresome chores at her parents' home in an upscale Chicago suburb, she hadn't done too badly this afternoon, she thought. The faint lemony scent and the bright interior of the apartment mutely testified to her efforts.

Nikki went into the kitchen, took out a package of baby carrots, and emptied them into a saucepan with a little water and a dab of margarine.

The baby carrots simmered with a low gurgle. When they were ready, she transferred them into a covered dish where they could be warmed up in the microwave later.

Nikki's work was finished and she felt the slow drag of tiredness which hadn't appeared until now. She pulled out one of the dining table chairs and sank into the emerald green luxury of its upholstery. Tired, she murmured to herself–she'd just lay her head on the table and shut her eyes for five minutes. She would hear when Mark came in and could then find out, once and for all, if he expected her to wait on him at dinnertime.

Female laughter and a deep male voice jarred Nikki awake. She opened her eyes, wondered where she was, and then suddenly remembered.

Mark and a tall, stunning brunette stood staring at her. Slowly, as she raised her head from the hard surface of the dining table, reality hit Nikki like a bucket of cold water thrown squarely in her face. Once again, she had fallen asleep in Mark's apartment, this time sitting in a chair.

"Well, if it isn't Sleeping Beauty! You didn't tell me you were living with someone, Mark." A hint of admonition seeped into the low breathy voice of the woman, who seemed unable to stand on her own power. She leaned against Mark like a decorative vine curving upward along the ramparts of a sturdy stone building.

"I...I must have dozed off." Nikki stood up, swaying a little. "Dinner's ready."

The woman arched a penciled eyebrow at Mark.

Nikki was aware of Mark's piercing gaze, all the more disconcerting because he hadn't said anything. He looked taller than she'd remembered. How tall was he? a disembodied voice shrilled in her head.

"This is Nikki Slater. She takes care of the apartment and the cooking." His voice was quiet and firm.

"Such a beautiful housekeeper," the woman crooned in a throaty voice, eyes narrowing as she studied Nikki with scrutinizing intensity.

Nikki ignored the woman. Guest or not, Mark was her employer. Her business was with him. "Would you like me to serve dinner?" she said.

"Lauren is staying for dinner." He had disengaged himself from the clutching hold of the woman, encouraging her to stand on her own and steadying her by the elbow. He turned to her now. "Or would you prefer to go out to eat?"

"Let's stay here. At least, we won't have to tip the waiter," Lauren said, giving Nikki a saccharin smile.

Nikki had the satisfaction of seeing Mark's lean features tighten and a muscle flick in his jaw. The remark was in poor taste, crass. Surely Mark saw that, too. And what did that say for the woman?

A dry chuckle rose silently in Nikki's throat. Such remarks from insensitive people were occupational hazards for her. Far from being stung, she pitied Lauren, who was apparently determined to claim Mark's attention. Mark, the international playboy. Yet...he didn't seem in the least bit cavalier in his manner.

"That all depends on whether Nikki is free to stay or not," Mark said.

"Of course, she'll stay. That's part of her job, isn't it?" Lauren sounded smug.

"I meant join us to eat dinner, Lauren," he said quietly.

"Well," Lauren said with a sniff. "That's a first...having the hired help to dinner."

Nikki went into the kitchen to set the table and bring out the dishes from the oven. She heard Mark follow close behind her.

"Would you like to stay for dinner?" he persisted.

She turned around holding up her mitt-clad hands and found herself facing him. Her gaze locked with his momentarily, and then she averted them. She could almost feel his breath on her–he was standing too close for her comfort.

She took a step back. "No. Thanks for asking."

She took the dish out of the oven and, holding it aloft, placed it on the dining table set for two. What sort of an employee did he take her for, crashing in on his *tete-a-tete* with a lady friend–or date?

"In that case, I'll leave the dishes in the sink and you can get them tomorrow." He assumed the tone an employer would use.

"Mark, how do you start the CD player?" Lauren called from the living room, giving the impression that she was bored from lack of attention.

"Be right there." He looked at Nikki. "Good night," he said. "See you bright and early tomorrow."

Nikki didn't know whether or not to be annoyed at his brusqueness. Perhaps her presence had intruded on whatever he had in mind with the lady friend, although what he saw in her, Nikki couldn't imagine. She'd never met a more brittle, superficial woman. Jealousy hit her like an invisible punch in the solar plexus. Nikki gasped. She *had* to get a hold on herself and remember Mark was only her employer!

She used the now-familiar archway entrance to her living

quarters and went home to look up recipes for tomorrow's cooking assignments. In the kitchen, she pulled out a large three-ring binder from under her tote bag on the kitchen table and leafed through it, marking a recipe for Veal Prince Orloff and another for cherry tort, and then put away the binder.

Shucking off her jeans and crumpled shirt, she wrapped a yellow chenille robe around herself and reveled in its soft texture. Curiously relaxed, she walked out onto the balcony.

Nikki held onto the railing and sniffed the lilac-scented air. The sound of a female voice drifted upward, forcing her to look down, and something made her grip the rail more tightly. Lauren and Mark were coming in to the parking area, Lauren clinging tightly to his arm. Mark's head seemed inclined toward her, but Nikki couldn't see his face. An unladylike word rose to her lips, raw envy holding her firmly in its grip like a metal claw. How she hated the feeling; it made her feel weak and out of control. Were they out on a date? Or perhaps he was just dropping her off.

Nikki abruptly turned and went back inside, shutting the balcony door. She had plenty to do without wondering how her employer was spending the rest of his evening. The sourness churning inside her wasn't making it easy for her to concentrate on her own chores. A shower first, she thought, and then she'd sort through her notes about location and inventory for when she would open her own catering service. It wouldn't hurt a bit to look into all that even now, instead of scrambling for it later—that way, she'd be able to compare her choices cost-wise. The thought of opening her own business invigorated her as always, and working toward it a little by little every day added meaning to her daily schedule. The idea of a cool shower beckoned to her, and she went for it like a fish searching for water. After all, it had been a long day.

Refreshed, Nikki wrapped the robe around her and sat at the dresser to untangle her hair with a comb, staring at the furrow on the forehead of her reflection. She'd done the best she could today, she reminded herself. Whether Mark thought so or not remained to be seen. She couldn't figure out in what spirit the invitation to stay to dinner had been extended to her this evening. Did he really think she'd join them?

Mark unlocked the apartment door and let himself in, mildly chafing at the time he'd lost entertaining Lauren and then taking her back to the hotel. He pushed the door shut with the sole of his foot and glanced at the short stack of dishes in the sink over which he'd dumped detergent and water so Nikki could tackle them in the morning. Opening the refrigerator, he saw Corning ware dishes in one corner of the middle shelf–leftovers for tomorrow's sandwiches. He wasn't much of an eater anyway. If only he could get back to his regular tennis schedule, but he'd been so busy lately.

Mark picked up the briefcase he'd hurriedly left near the sofa earlier. He wanted to see if Nikki had completed all the housework. This job was no easy street for her, he'd make sure of that!

He shook his head as the persistent little suspicion jogged into his mind again. If Nikki had corralled Gran into negotiating this job so she could have it easy while raking in a fairly sizeable paycheck, he'd make sure to remedy that in short order.

Now for his bi-weekly call to Gran. Mark deposited his briefcase on the study table and, picking up the cell phone, dialed the number.

"Hello, Gran?" he said.

"How's my favorite grandson?"

He smiled at the elation in her voice. His grandmother sounded energetic. Lately, he'd worried that she'd been too involved in her charity work, because every time he called she was on her way out to some fundraiser. But she loved that sort of thing—it gave her life a mission.

"I'm fine. The new housekeeper's arrived," he began cautiously, wondering how to broach the subject of Nikki. "Do you know her well?"

A brief pause followed. "I've known her since I joined cooking classes. About a year."

"I see. I just wondered if she was another hard-luck case you're too goodhearted to resist."

"Mark, you should know me better than that. I know I've made some mistakes helping the wrong people in the past, but Nikki isn't one of them."

"I just don't want somebody taking advantage of your trusting nature, that's all." Mark wasn't completely convinced that Ellen knew how to resist the down-and-out people she forever ran into.

"At least now I'll know you're eating right," Ellen said with a laugh. "Did you just get home from the office?"

"Actually, Marnie's brother's daughter is in town and I invited her to dinner. Just dropped her back at the hotel." As a favor to his father, he added in a mental footnote. Anything to keep him happy in his new marriage. A sigh escaped against his will.

"That was nice of you." His grandmother sounded genuinely pleased. But if he knew her at all, she'd have the dynamics of the situation well in hand—she knew how Marnie, the ex-showgirl from Las Vegas, manipulated his father. "You're a good son. If Otis weren't so busy, he'd have time to appreciate it. You just make sure you have a life and don't wear yourself out working in that tenth floor office of yours."

It had been a while since Mark had heard her talk like this. He shook his head. His grandmother felt his father, ambitious as he was, needed to touch base with him more, but Mark didn't mind. After all, he wasn't a kid whose parents needed to attend all his baseball games and other school functions. In fact, the private school he'd attended was his home away from home, which was all to the good for Otis. It allowed him his business trips after taking that long proverbial sigh of relief.

"Do you know Nikki's family background?" Mark asked. He had to make sure it didn't slip his mind in all the chatter.

"She doesn't say much. But I do know she's hardworking and ambitious. She plans to open a catering service after finishing her training," Ellen said, sounding quite content with her understanding of the young woman she'd befriended. Mark didn't want to sound like the town naysayer–he thought he'd better keep his reservations about Nikki to himself and watch her closely.

Mark wandered out to the dining room with the phone and his eye caught the oven mittens Nikki had left on the counter. He couldn't expel a mental picture of her standing there with an apron and mittens, too pretty to be a domestic. There went the thump in his gut again, just thinking of her.

"Are you there, Mark?" His grandmother's voice jerked him back to the present.

"Er–yes. Still here. I'd better go, I have some contracts to look through for tomorrow." He said goodnight and snapped the phone shut.

Mark enjoyed phone conversations with his grandmother. She was his one link to sanity-ever since he could remember, he'd spent the best days of his life at her comfortable house with its old-fashioned furniture and lived-in look. He remembered how she used to read to him at bedtime when his mother was still living. Yes, he'd owe Ellen a lot even if she weren't his grandmother, which was why he'd make darned sure Nikki wasn't taking advantage of her.

He started unbuttoning his shirt. A shower would be great, and then he'd take his papers and laptop to bed with him and start working. He grinned to himself. Talk of the hectic social life of a bachelor! This was more like detention, except he didn't think of his work as detention. He loved it, loved creating and working with the construction people and attorneys, and advising clients as to what was best for them, giving them the best product for their money.

Half an hour later, showered, toweled, and clad in shorts and an old T-shirt, Mark leaned back against the pillows and studied the papers spread out all over the bed, the laptop balancing in his lap.

He glanced around the room. For the first time, he noticed that his clothes had been folded away, his brush and change tray where he'd want them. He grinned, thinking of Nikki's hands touching his T-shirts and shorts as she sorted through them, giving him a feeling of sly satisfaction. The thoughts that raced through his mind at this moment would cause the most brazen stripper to blush—he'd have given anything to know how Nikki would react to what he was thinking now. Ha!

Mark's grin vanished as he thought of how Nikki had declined his dinner invitation. She didn't react as he expected. This girl was either legitimate, which he doubted, or a better con artist than he'd imagined, which meant his grandmother was being fooled, and Mark didn't like the feeling of hopeless dread that bombarded him at the thought. How could he convince Gran she was being hoodwinked into thinking her protégé was on the level? She thought Nikki was a sweet innocent. Sweet she might be, but innocent? Mark couldn't believe that.

CHAPTER THREE

Mark looked across the boardroom at the mid-morning haze on the Loop. From the tenth floor the vehicles reminded him of matchbox cars inching along like flat, slow-moving dominoes.

He took a sip of coffee from the dark blue mug marked "Runyon Architects and Engineers," and winced. Because Lois, his secretary, had come in late this morning, he'd had to make the coffee, which tasted and looked like tar.

The directors' meeting about the Renaissance Court seniors' condos had gone well, especially in light of the ongoing expansion project commissioned by the O'Hare Airport Authority. Their manpower resources had been stretched tight, but their superior team of architects and engineers had done the Runyon name proud. During the two-hour session, they'd discussed the several phases of construction for the proposed seniors' condo. A great central location was one of the reasons the older apartment building had been demolished, and Nikki had bounded into his life as a result.

Mark's grip tightened over the mug as he remembered going home over the last few weeks to find Nikki cleaning and making dinner. The more he saw of her, the less she reminded him of the usual run of housekeepers. And how was a man to keep his mind on scale models and cost projections when a shapely woman with a cloth duster tucked in her waistband went by, carrying with her the faint whiff of some perfume? Why couldn't she just cook and leave like Mrs. Babbitt used to? He knew the answer to that—because she needed a place to stay near the cooking school.

Mark had watched her closely to gauge her work performance. The slightest indication of unwillingness or laziness would confirm his ever-present suspicions, but so far, he couldn't find anything to complain about. Could he be wrong? No, there was something not quite right about Nikki—she didn't ring true.

He felt his forehead furrow as he remembered her rolling the vacuum cleaner past him, carrying a caddy of cleansers in the other hand and acting as if he weren't there. Could that only be a pretense to show him that she took her work seriously? He looked up as a knock on the door pulled him away from his thoughts. An intense-looking, thirty-something man wearing thick glasses walked in holding a massive sheaf of papers. Mark grinned at him. Dave Roth kept a bird's-eye-view hold on all simultaneous projects with the talent of a juggler's precision, saving Mark a few ulcers.

"We've managed to find apartments for all the residents of the Nob Hill building at last report from Ted Carling," Dave said, putting down the papers temporarily and leaning against the conference table. "At least all those who wanted assistance in finding one."

"Less one," Mark muttered to himself.

"Pardon?"

"Oh—er," Mark said, looking away in embarrassment. "I ran into somebody who told me she was done out of her convenient-location apartment because of our plans to put up the new condo."

Luckily, Dave did not seem to notice Mark's sudden unease.

"Really? Does she want to be accommodated too?"

"No. She's made other arrangements." Mark didn't see any need to tell Dave the details of the whole untidy story of how Nikki was now his housekeeper.

The intercom buzzed from Lois' office, and Mark pressed an orange button. "Yes?"

"An overseas call from Dahram–a Prince Khalid." Doubt mixed with an edge of curiosity came through in Lois' voice. "Not *the* Prince Khalid?"

"Yes, we had consulted on the design for their airport before you were hired."

"He's coming to the States and plans to stop here to see you. A real prince."

Mark chuckled at the dreamy sound of her voice. "Hold on to your keyboard, Lois. He's really a down-to-earth guy, no big deal."

"For you, maybe," Lois muttered. "I'll put him through," she said before going off the intercom.

A clipped Eton accent came over the line. "Hello, sport."

"Hello, yourself," Mark said. "Hear you're planning a visit to the States."

"Yes. All right with you?"

"More than all right," Mark replied. "I'd like to have you come to dinner at my place."

"As you Americans say, '*now* you're talkin'" Prince Khalid replied, affecting an American accent.

Mark threw back his head and laughed. They chatted for a few minutes more before hanging up. Dave, listening in on the conversation, came to life. "Are we rolling out the red carpet?" he asked.

"No need for that. He's pretty informal despite all the pomp and splendor he's used to in his own country."

Mark remembered the royal treatment *he'd* been given when visiting Dahram on business. After seeing nothing but miles of sand and working with the civil engineers, the prince had seen to it that Mark was kept entertained at night, complete with sumptuous banquets and exotic belly dancing.

The last time the prince had come to the States, he'd spent an evening in Mark's apartment playing video games and sipping chocolate malt.

"Let me know if we're going to make any special arrangements for his visit," Dave said.

"You'll be the first to know."

That seemed to satisfy Dave, and he hefted the sheaf of papers back into his arms. "Off to check out some dimensions," he said, and walked out with his usual purposeful stride.

Mark grabbed his coffee mug and strode into the large adjoining room that served as his office. Its book-lined ambience provided just the atmosphere he needed to get things done. Tall shelves contained thick books on code regulations, standing reliable and ready like soldiers on call. A side table held two computers, and his desk was strewn with invoices, contract papers, and a collection of black binders.

He sank into the shiny leather swivel chair and sorted through the sheets on his desk, signing off on some of them with a ballpoint pen.

"There. How do you like that?"

Nikki stared at her reflection in the lighted mirror of her friend Jenn's beauty salon. "I like it a lot."

"The highlights and a bit of trimming bring out your pert

features. Face it, you've got model-type looks," Jenn said.

"Then why am I working as a housekeeper?"

"Because you're stubborn and insist on supporting yourself." Jenn pretended to look serious. "Actually, you're doing an admirable job. But then, you were independent even as a kid. My mother always thought so, too."

"If it weren't for your mother, and you and your brothers, I'd never have known what a happy family life was," Nikki said lightly, trying to keep regret from her voice. No use dwelling on what she lacked as a child. She'd only sound like a poor little rich girl.

"So what's this guy like? Don't tell me he actually thinks you're a for-real domestic," Jenn said with a smirk.

Nikki grinned. "He hasn't a clue about me. He thinks I corralled Ellen into getting me an easy job."

"Maybe you should let your employer know your folks are rich. That way he won't think you took advantage of his grandmother to get you a comfortable job." Jenn whipped the plastic cover off Nikki's shoulders and aimed two short bolts of hair spray at the shiny golden head.

"That would be worse–then he'd think I don't need the money, which I do, and that I'm doing it on a strange whim. What would that say about me as a professional cook and housekeeper? Besides, where I'm from is not any of his business. It's not a 'comfortable' job, as you call it. I can cook. The cleaning I don't know about."

"How would you? Your parents always had a houseful of domestic help," her friend said.

Nikki grimaced. "I'm learning. It's not as hard as I thought it'd be." She studied her reflection and pushed back her chair. "Thanks. This'll hold me for a while."

Jenn put away scissors and combs. "I have a half hour

before my next customer. Come in the back and have some coffee."

"Love to. My cooking demo went well and I deserve a break before heading for work." Nikki followed her friend to the back of the salon where hair products of every kind lined the room on tall, gray metal shelves.

"How about sharing a chicken salad with me?" Jenn said. "I'd better grab lunch; it's now or never."

Nikki nodded. "I'm famished."

They sat with two bowls of salad and mugs of steaming hot coffee.

Jenn looked up. "You could help me around here if your housekeeping job doesn't work out."

A look of bewilderment crossed Nikki's face. She shook her head. "I couldn't. You know the old saying about mixing business and friendship. I rely on your friendship, Jenn. I'll be okay–really." She hoped. She had to be okay–the money helped her keep her head afloat and pay a few bills.

"But if he's a tyrant..."

"I don't have him figured out yet, but he does seem picky, set in his ways. Doesn't pay compliments easily."

Jenn gave her friend a knowing look. "I'm going to keep an eye on you, girl."

"You do that." Nikki got up and put her bowl and mug in the sink. "Thanks for lunch. I have to go." She gave Jenn a hug and walked out to her car.

Nikki drove out of the mini-mall where Jenn had her beauty salon and headed straight for Tivoli Apartments. She couldn't think of it as "home," just temporary camping until she set up her own business and found a nice apartment nearby.

She had to hurry. Mark was bringing a special guest today–a prince from Dahram, he'd said. Nikki conjured up a picture of a portly potentate sitting on a brocade-covered divan, watching dancing girls and smoking a gurgling hookah, like the brightly colored drawings in the *Arabian Nights* book she'd read as a child. The way Mark had talked about him, it sounded as if they were not only business associates but also good friends.

She parked her car under the building and took the elevator up to stash her purse and tote bag in her apartment before going to Mark's place to start the cleaning. When Nikki reached the fourth floor, she felt like somebody had socked her in the gut. In front of Mark's apartment stood two tall men dressed in black trench coats. At the sight of her, one of them automatically placed his hand inside his trench coat as if concealing a six-shooter.

"Excuse me, miss," said the other man. He held up a silver identification badge embedded in a black leather pouch. "We're Embassy Security. His Royal Highness Prince Khalid is in Mr. Runyon's apartment. Do you live in the adjoining one?"

Nikki's jaw fell open. The next moment, she pulled herself together. "Yes, and I also work for him."

"And you are?"

"Nikki Slater."

"Some identification please."

Nikki fumbled in her cavernous tote bag and then held up her driver's license.

"Please proceed. Sorry to have detained you, but we have orders to interview everyone who uses this floor." The man took a step back and appeared to relax.

Nikki went into her apartment and blew out a breath. How was she going to get the cleaning done, if His Royal Highness The Prince was in Mark's apartment?

She had cleaned thoroughly yesterday, she had even found a short stepladder and washed the chandeliers with soapy water until they sparkled like rhinestones under an arc lamp, but she still had to pick up papers and clothes left from Mark's hurried departure for work this morning. After serving breakfast as usual, she'd set out on her day intending to return later and tackle the cleaning.

Doing her job and attending cooking classes required intrepid juggling skills to keep both viable. But, although her head sometimes ached from concentrating and her legs felt wobbly from racing around so much, deep down she had the satisfaction of getting closer to her dream of opening her own catering service and being her own boss.

Nikki left her purse on the bedroom dresser and hurried to Mark's apartment through the connecting door. She should have tried to get in earlier; she could have had the lamb roast done and picked up around the apartment before Mark and his guest arrived.

How did one behave in the presence of royalty? She couldn't be held liable for any lapses of protocol since she was only the lowly hired help. Nikki chuckled as she turned the gleaming brass knob and let herself in.

Male voices drifted from the living room—Mark's deep one and a more crisp tone. A moment later, the men came into view. Mark stood holding a can of pop; at the sight of Nikki the guest stood up. Neat and compact in build, short, muscular, and light-skinned, he wore dark pants with a polo T-shirt. Nikki could envision him driving a polo stick on horseback admirably in chukka after chukka—as a child, she'd watched with her mother as her father played polo at the Naperville Polo Club in Oak Brook.

"We have a guest for dinner today," Mark said

smoothly–too smoothly, it seemed, because a vein throbbed visibly at his temple. She could sense the approaching storm. He was mad at her for sauntering in late.

"I'd like to see you in the kitchen about the menu." Though he spoke smoothly, his face looked too ruddy for her own comfort. He was obviously annoyed because she wasn't here when they arrived; clearly, he'd expected to find her laying the table to the succulent aroma of something roasting in the oven or being delicately fried.

Nikki felt his measured tread close behind her. Here it comes, she thought, the court martial for not being on the job. And it was not just his controlled annoyance she felt, there was something else–the magnetic pull he seemed to wield. For a nanosecond she wanted him to think well of her. The next minute she wondered why.

She turned around. "Before you say anything, I want to say I meant to be here much sooner, but..." She daren't say she had stopped at Jenn's to get her hair touched up. That would be like signing her death warrant which, in this case, wouldn't be as bad as losing her job.

"I was delayed at the Institute," she said finally. "They were having a demo by a guest lecturer from France." Which was true; the class had been treated to a presentation of French desserts–Chocolate Fondue and Crepes Chantilly.

Nikki glanced quickly at the thundercloud that was threatening to erupt on Mark's face. She needn't try telling him about crepes and fondues when he was in battle mode!

"I told you about the prince's visit two weeks ago," he said.

"I know you told me, but it slipped my mind today."

"Slipped your mind!"

"The lamb is thawing in the refrigerator. It won't take

long to prepare dinner and a dessert." Nikki grabbed her apron and tied it around her waist. For a moment his gaze seemed to linger at her waist, then his eyes garnered their earlier thundercloud quality, and she could feel herself come thudding down to earth faster than a parachuting astronaut.

"Well, then, you'd better get started on it. The prince is looking forward to a good meal. He said he had had only breakfast today. So," Mark said, backing out of the kitchen, "it had better be good."

Nikki opened the refrigerator, took out the lamb, and started to prepare it. Mark's obvious irritation had unsettled her, but she was going to lay out such a spread that they would never forget it.

She heard bellowing laughter from the living room as she whipped up a delicate marinade of lemon juice, garlic sauce, and cooking wine to pour over the shoulder of lamb. There would be asparagus in a white sauce and potatoes roasted in butter and dill, then to finish it off, she would serve up her signature cherry tort.

Before too long, a delectable aroma filled the kitchen. It was time to set out the dinnerware and she got busy, shunting between kitchen and dining room.

When Mark had told her about the prince's visit, she had bought special bread from an ethnic food store so he would feel right at home. And Mark...she'd be fooling herself if she didn't know that this display was also for his benefit.

"Dinner is served," Nikki announced, walking into the living room where the men sat looking at a model of a high-rise building Mark had placed on the coffee table. For all the world, they looked like two boys playing with Lego blocks, and she nearly choked trying to quell a chuckle. The price and size of their toys were the only difference between men and boys, as the old saying went.

They looked up at her. "Yes?" Tiny lines furrowed Mark's forehead.

Had he forgotten it was dinnertime? Maybe she should have taken longer until they were really hungry. That way, her cooking would win, hands down.

"Dinner's served." Nikki noticed the prince's gaze transfixed on her. She should have been flattered by his disarming stare, but at the moment she only wanted dinner to proceed with the smoothness of a well-oiled door hinge.

"Thank you," Mark said and turned to the prince. "Shall we?"

Going into the dining room, they seated themselves and waited to be served. Nikki placed pieces of roast lamb neatly sliced onto each plate and then stood by.

"In my country, there is a saying that every man can be a king if he is a guest in another's house. Mark, this is a great honor. I have never seen such a loaded table since my father's sixty-fifth birthday bash."

Mark laughed. "There goes your elegant hyperbole. But thanks, I'm flattered. That is, Nikki, our intrepid chef here, is responsible for this spread."

"I hope you like what I've prepared." Nikki removed the lid from the dish of small, glazed golden brown potatoes fried whole and lightly garnished with dill.

"This is excellent lamb," Khalid said, engrossed in maneuvering a piece on his plate with extreme concentration.

"Glad you like it, Your Highness," Nikki said.

He held up a hand. "Please, no titles here. Call me Khalid. And, Nikki, next time Mark comes to Dahram, you must come, too. You can hold a special demonstration of American cuisine at the palace." He nodded at Mark, who looked as if he had just been bopped on the head with a pan. "Is that a deal, my friend?'

The familiar thundercloud expression was starting to form on Mark's face like a flock of rooks descending on a hilltop. "That's certainly something to think about," he said.

Nikki edged away to make space for more dishes on the sideboard. Mark had yet to compliment her cooking. Did he like it? He wasn't saying. She flushed with mild annoyance at his apparent disregard for her culinary skills. Why couldn't he bring himself to give her one compliment? Was that asking too much?

Half an hour later, the plates were cleared away.

"Ready for dessert?" Nikki brought out the cherry tort in crystal dessert plates with shiny silverware.

Khalid beamed at Nikki. "This is too much. I feel sorry for my older brother. He's the heir to the throne, you know, and doesn't get to travel as much as I do," he said in a confidential tone that amused Nikki.

"Poor guy, he must have it hard," Mark said, a smile curving his mouth.

"My younger brother, on the other hand, is ready to visit the States." Khalid raised large, soulful eyes at Nikki. "Americans are so lucky. You can marry whom you choose."

Mark cleared his throat, pushed his chair back, and picked up his cherry tort with a zig-zag motion.

"Sometimes there's the question of making the right choice," Mark said, glaring at his plate.

Nikki caught her breath at the edge in his tone, controlled though it was. What was he thinking about? Had there been someone in Mark's life who had hurt him? Is that why he was so suspicious of her?

She gathered the plates, returned to the kitchen and, after

stacking the dishes in the sink, began to make coffee.

Returning to the dining room, she found the men had left the table and had adjourned to the living room to look at printouts of something. Building plans?

"Ready for coffee?" Nikki said.

"No, thank you." The prince raised his hand.

"I'll have to pass too," Mark said.

"A sumptuous dinner, Miss Slater."

"Call me Nikki, please," she said with a smile, unsure if she had crossed the boundaries of royal protocol. Nah–Prince Khalid didn't seem the traditional example of a standoffish member of royalty.

"Mark, enough of these dry building plans," Khalid said with a laugh. "You're the expert. I leave any future recommendations to you, and my father trusts my decisions." He crossed his legs and leaned back on the sofa. "So, Nikki, Mark tells me you're studying catering to start your own business."

Nikki felt the electric surge of Mark's gaze piercing her. She held her breath. "It's something I've always wanted to do."

"I admire that," Prince Khalid said. "Going out into the world and making your own destiny. We have to educate our people to move from a fatalistic mind set. Of course, with the tradition of centuries, it's hard to know where custom ends and superstition begins. But enough of that." He stood up. "It's time I left for the Embassy."

"Glad you took time from your busy schedule to come here, Khalid." Mark shook hands with him. "I'll tell the guys waiting outside."

"I do hope you will consider our invitation to visit Dahram, Nikki." He extended his hand.

Nikki extended hers thinking he was going to shake it.

Instead, he raised it and gently kissed it with the hint of a bow. Charming, she thought.

"Thank you, Your Highness," Nikki said turning away just in time to see an amused smirk on Mark's face. "I may just take you up on that offer."

A wicked bravado surged through her. If Mark insisted on being suspicious, she'd make sure she expressed her admiration of the prince.

"Let me know what you want on the new proposal," Mark said striding toward the door. He appeared to have summoned his composure after witnessing the gallantry which he, no doubt, relegated to ballet performances and stage plays.

"I will. And thank you for your hospitality."

Mark held the door open and the prince stepped into the brightly lit hallway. The Security men materialized out of nowhere to escort the royal guest back to his Embassy.

It took a good ten minutes for Mark to say anything. Nikki returned to the kitchen to clean up, feeling buoyed up by the prince's arrival and departure, and his obvious pleasure in her company. How nice it felt to be appreciated and not be under a cloud of suspicion!

"Well, I hope you're satisfied." Mark strode into the kitchen, his face tauter than usual.

"Satisfied?" Nikki was puzzled. What was he talking about?

"You made a spectacle of yourself, parading in front of Khalid," Mark said, stopping her in between the dining room and kitchen.

"Spectacle? What do you mean?"

Uh-oh, she thought. He'd been quiet, watching her all during the time she and the prince were chattering. She'd even noticed a muscle working fiercely in his jaw, but she'd enjoyed the easygoing camaraderie of the prince so much that she forgot all about protocol, or whatever it was called. Could Mark be jealous? The thought suddenly gave her a surge of pleasure. Mark jealous! What an exciting possibility.

"You could have compromised security."

"Whose? Mine? On the contrary, he seemed perfectly well-behaved. A gentleman." Nikki couldn't resist the remark, or the chuckle that rose in her throat.

"I couldn't agree with you more. Fortunately, he's a friend of mine, so I ought to know, which is more than I can say about you."

"That I'm not a gentleman?" The prodding remark appealed to her no end.

"A lady." His mouth set in a grim line and he stared at her.

"Now how would you know what a lady is, judging by the women you take out?" There, she'd said it! Nikki turned to leave, but he caught her arm.

"What do you mean by that?" His hand on her arm was firm and his gaze bored deeply into her eyes. "Let me tell you something, I make my own choices in women and I won't be railroaded into it."

Again the suspicious look on his face. She would have loved to know where that came from. And what could he have meant by that remark?

"Don't worry, I'm not about to trap you if that's what you're afraid of," Nikki said.

He let go of her arm and took a step back. "Here's one for you. I'm not about to let you." A wry smile flitted across his face, sending Nikki's heart into a thud.

"Fine!"

"Fine!"

Nikki strode into the kitchen, her mouth set tightly as a precaution against saying anything she might later regret. She heard Mark stride into the living room and, from what she could hear, he was in a big huff. So far they had that in common!

"I hope that grandson of mine appreciates what a fine cook you are, Nikki dear." Ellen sipped her tea reflectively.

They sat on the open deck of the Saunders Institute where chairs and tables were placed for people who wanted to bring their lunch. Nikki had never seen so many people outside, despite the dripping stickiness of the weather—a cooling breeze lifted off the lake now and then, and she bunched up her hair and stuck bobby pins in it, feeling the curly mop with her fingers.

"Er—you know how men are. They won't compliment a woman except under life-and-death situations," Nikki said lightly, trying to ignore the crunch in the pit of her stomach.

"If your menus are anything like the sumptuous turnouts in class, I know my grandson is eating right." Ellen rummaged in her shoulder bag and brought out a white paper bag of cherries. "Have some Bing cherries, my dear. They say these are good for something or other—I can't remember what."

Nikki plucked a few and jammed them in her mouth, remembering the fiasco with the prince. Mark's jaw had gotten harder by the minute after Prince Khalid left and they went back in to clean up. Ellen thrust the paper bag in her direction. "Have some more. You look a little peaked." She peered at her, then fumbled for her glasses and put them on.

"That's because I was up half the night looking for a suitable recipe for today's surprise bakeoff. And before that, I was cleaning my apartment which had started looking like a pigsty at feeding time."

That was only half the truth. She'd gone back in the afternoon yesterday so that there would be no repeat of the incident when the prince had showed up with his host, and the housekeeper had wandered in later wearing a dazed look. She had dashed back to mop, clean, brush, and dust before Mark had another bright idea of bringing clients home.

"That's what I like about you. You are conscientious about keeping things neat. Look at you, not a hair out of place in this choking heat"

Nikki laughed. "Correction. Do you see the mess on my head? That's my hair. And my skirt and blouse are a disgrace, sticking to me the way they are."

She stood up and shook out her skirt until people around her stared.

"I'm glad you like the job. You *do* like it, don't you?"

"Of course." The chasing around was driving her crazier than a beaver looking for logs to dam a stream, but darned if she'd admit that to Ellen. She needed the job for the chef it was turning her into, and the money wasn't exactly peanuts either.

"I'm learning more about everything that I missed all these years. No better way to learn than the hard way." Nikki took a quick breath. Ellen mustn't misunderstand or she'd think Nikki couldn't handle the workload. "It builds character," she said smiling, "and muscle."

"And you have plenty of character," Ellen sighed. "You remind me of my daughter, a busy headstrong girl just like you. She up and married Otis even when I warned her against it. She listened for exactly one minute, then went her own way."

"Otis is Mark's father?" Nikki stiffened with interest, every muscle and nerve standing at attention. "What's he like?"

"Ambitious, energetic. Loves Mark in his own way, but

never seemed to have time. What with his contracts and marriage to Marnie," Ellen shook her head. "It isn't like Mark to complain. He never did even as a little boy."

Nikki grinned at the thought of Mark as a little boy. He must have been headstrong too. He'd have something of his mother in him.

"He seems very fond of you, Ellen." Nikki remembered the softening of his features when he spoke of his grandmother. She could say, "He just can't connect me up with you without thinking that I somehow talked you into giving me this job," but that would distress Ellen. She'd have an ear-busting talk with Mark, and that would be the end of Nikki's job, her prospects, and her life, which was starting to rev up with her in the driver's seat.

"He's a dear boy, but hard to understand. If he can tolerate me at all, it's because I spent the most time with him when he grew up except when he went to private school and then college."

Nikki smiled at the thought of Mark as "a dear boy." How did he think of himself–God's gift to women and the architectural world? She'd watch him closely; she wasn't taking any chances, which was why she kept up this breakneck pace of work, study, and housekeeping every day.

"I know you think it's funny, but he'll always be my little boy." Ellen's eyes glowed with what could only be affection–it burst onto her face like flashing beacon.

"You'll have to excuse me, it simply wouldn't be right to think of one's employer as 'dear boy.' Might come in the way of harmonious employee relations." Nikki patted Ellen on the hand and grabbed a few more cherries. She glanced at her watch, which showed two-thirty. Today she could leave early, having been here since seven in the morning for the bakeoff and then classes.

"Going dear?" Ellen stood up and gave her a hug. "See you bright and early tomorrow."

Nikki ran down to her car with a feeling of escape. As dearly as she loved Ellen, she couldn't have her making remarks that she looked "peaked" and wonder if the job was giving her the heebie jeebies. Meaning well, she'd call Mark and scold him about it! Then Nikki might as well say goodbye to her plans—all of them in one fell swoop.

CHAPTER FOUR

Nikki's gaze darted toward the darkening scene outside. A blinding bolt of lightning zig-zagged across the sky, followed by a deafening clap of thunder.

The large kitchen in Mark's apartment was filled with the aroma of seasoned wild rice, while beef and vegetable stir-fry sizzled noisily in an oversized wok. Another deep rumble of thunder burst like a sonic boom, and Nikki clapped her hands to her ears.

She remembered as a child that, when her parents were away, she used to pull the bedcovers over her head at night at the sound of thunder. But she was a big girl now—couldn't let a little thunder get to her.

Despite the hissing and whizzing of the cooking—the test of an excellent chef—Nikki heard the clunking and rapping of the keyboard from the den where Mark worked. Her ears pricked up. No clients today, or even a last-minute after-hours meeting with his planning team. Mark had walked in early today and had nearly bumped into a bucket of water which stood ready for Nikki to mop the floor.

"Watch where you're going," she'd called out.

"Be a lot safer if you didn't make this place an obstacle course." Mark sidestepped the offending bucket and dropped his briefcase and laptop on the hall table.

"I'm nearly finished here. It's about five-thirty now, do

you want dinner?" Nikki made sure there was just the right touch of formality. She wouldn't play the wife receiving the husband home after a hard day at the office, although at times that fantasy had invaded her mind, which was one of the reasons she fought it so hard.

Mark put a hand to his back, flexed it, and then straightened. Picking up his things from the hall table, he said, "Yes, I'm starved," and headed toward the den.

Nikki whipped off her apron and went to set the table in the dining room, but Mark beat her to it. He was spreading out what looked like large shiny photo prints of mockups of buildings–scale models? He stood there, hand to hip, the chandelier light glossing his thick hair and unaware that Nikki was approaching in soft-soled shoes.

He'd changed into jeans and a blue oxford shirt. From where she stood, he looked an absolute knockout. She deserved a good shaking for even thinking those undesirable thoughts and chalked them up to her treadmill schedule and her lack of a life. A life! When had she ever had one? After serving dinner, she had to clean her apartment, then transcribe the notes she'd taken on the elegant *Pot Roast Provencale* demo she'd attended at cooking class that morning. Now, *there* was a dish that gave universal pleasure!

Mark looked up, a vacant expression on his face. Obviously, she was no comparison to whatever he was gaping at spread out on the table; not that she was trying to get his attention, but there was something terribly dampening to the ego when an attractive man didn't notice a woman's presence.

"Time to set the table," she said lightly, trying to show she was unaffected by him. "Would you like me to help you clear those papers off the table?" Was that the right touch of indifference and deference as an employee and working-girl-with-a-mission?

"Actually, I need these papers here. You can use the kitchen table to serve dinner," Mark replied, and returned to staring at his work.

Miffed, Nikki returned to the kitchen. At least he could try and make conversation, she thought, since they were practically neighbors and considering her tight schedule. But then, why would he care that she was spreading herself so thin. Was this how "for real" housewives felt? No wonder they ranted and raved when their husbands came home in the evening, "*You don't talk to me, and after I slaved over a hot stove all day.*" There I go again, expecting too much from him, she thought. After all, he was just an employer.

Today, determination pushed her forward. She'd finish up here and be free to do whatever she wanted for the rest of the evening. Nikki laid the table, then transferred the wild rice and stir-fry beef into serving dishes, and placed them on the table.

Suddenly, there was another clash of thunder. It had stopped for a while and Nikki forgot about it, assuming gratefully that that was the end of the deafening rumbles overhead. But this time, the lights flickered and then...total blackout.

"Oh, no," Nikki groaned. "Not now." She had too much to do, and this could last an eternity. She strained her ears, but there was total silence. What was Mark doing in the dining room?

"Nikki, are you alright back there?"

She heard his voice clearly. Surprise kept her silent. This was the first time he'd called her by name and it sounded...sweet, making her feel tingly all over. Come to think of it, he didn't call her anything–not "Miss Slater," not "miss,"–nothing.

"Yes," Nikki called back. "Do you have a flashlight?"

No response for a few minutes. Had he lost his way and would she have to rescue him?

Nikki felt her way back to the kitchen counter. The pitch-black room made her feel claustrophobic, the way she sometimes did in an elevator. Oh, she hated blackouts! The only thing worse than a blackout was thunder and lightening.

Then she heard footsteps and saw a dimly moving light from beyond the kitchen. Mark had found something that produced light. Thank goodness. At least, she wouldn't feel throttled by the dark.

"Coming through," he said. "Take your pick. I have candles, a large outdoor flashlight, and a penlight torch." The powerful flashlight he carried under his arm illuminated his face, giving it an interesting glow. He had several other gizmos clutched in his hand.

Nikki took two thick candles from him. "Do you have a match to light these?"

"In my pocket. I grabbed some from the supplies drawer in the den."

"Dinner is ready. I just have to set out the food." Nikki moved to the counter.

"Did you have plans for the evening when you get done here?"

The question whacked her on the head, coming as it did out of the blue.

"I...er...I was going to clean my apartment and do a few other things." *Catch up on sleep, do the laundry, wonder what to fix for dinner.*

"Tell you what. Why don't you stay and have dinner with me?" Mark grinned at her. "In fact, I wish you would."

Alone with him? In the dark? "Oh, no, I couldn't."

Totally unprepared, Nikki wanted to escape as gracefully as she could. "I have things to do."

"I can't stop you from going, but I'd like for you to stay. I've been so busy all these weeks that a blackout seems to be somebody's way of telling me to slow down."

The flickering candle shone on his lean, handsome features. Eyebrows lifted in a question. "What do you say?"

The charge of his attraction pushed her into accepting the invitation. Just this once, it wouldn't matter, would it?

"Thank you. Yes, I'd like that. Would you like to give me a hand with the food?"

"Yes, ma'am. I've done some camping in earlier days, so I'm not a complete klutz at culinary arts. Not as artsy as you, being in cooking school, but passable."

Nikki came out from behind the counter. "This is the first time I've ever heard you say anything about yourself. Actually, anything at all."

"I'm not one for talking about myself." Mark picked up the dishes from the counter. "Besides, the Senior Citizens' condo is taking off and I'm busy with that."

"Oh, the condo." That was why she was here in the first place, but she no longer felt the anger of being put out of her apartment–and that surprised her.

"I know you'll never forgive me for ousting you and your fellow residents from that building," Mark said, "but it did not meet certain requirements. For one thing, it was too old and did not meet the updated fire code. Being in that choice location, the company is better off putting up a new state-of-the-art structure."

"Try telling that to the residents," Nikki said casually. It was now an old story and it did not rankle. Was she softening just a tad?

Mark took his seat and Nikki took hers opposite him. The thick lavender-scented candle gave off a soft fragrance and they helped themselves to the food in the shadows cast by the flickering flame. Nikki unfolded her cloth napkin. It felt surrealistic to be sitting here chatting with this man, who was the cause of such a shift in her lifestyle.

"I know, and you're not going to let me forget it." Mark forked a piece of broccoli into his mouth. "Someday you'll see the merits of doing what we had to do with that building, then you'll understand." He set his fork down and looked at her, his gaze holding her in its steady grip.

Nikki's pulse hammered erratically. In front of her sat a man who could very easily be taken for JFK Jr.'s double, and she was supposed to put food into her mouth as if she needed sustenance.

Nikki lay her fork down, suddenly losing her appetite. She hadn't had time to eat anything besides some fruit for lunch, and she couldn't remember if she'd had any breakfast. But for the life of her, she couldn't eat another bite. The intimacy of candlelight and sitting across a table from Mark made her self-conscious. Her throat constricted and she couldn't swallow.

"What's the matter? Why aren't you eating?" His gorgeous dark eyes melted on her again, and confusion raked through her like a knife at her thoughts. She was darned if she would ever let on that she found him attractive. She had lost her composure momentarily and perhaps he had noticed. Not good at all.

"Oh, I am." Nikki quickly picked up her fork again. "How's the food?"

A few moments crawled by, moments that seemed like an eternity to Nikki while he decided. He nodded. "Not bad," he said finally and took a sip of water.

"Not bad? That's it?"

Obviously, he had no knowledge of the finer points of gourmet cooking. Monkeys in a zoo would show more appreciation of good cooking. She pushed away a feeling of irritation at his cavalier attitude to her cooking.

"I'm not a food person. To me, it keeps body and soul together. Sometimes I eat only a large bowl of cereal for dinner, especially if I'm working at home." He grinned at her. "That surprise you?"

"Not really. Ellen hinted you weren't eating right. And she wanted me to make sure you did. That's part of my contract with her for getting me a job and a place to stay."

"Of course." His expression hardened suddenly as if suspicion had entered his mind. What was he thinking? "And that's why you're here."

Mark was probably indulging in his theory that she made friends with Ellen only to get the job, but she wasn't going to let that affect her.

Nikki looked up and smiled sweetly. "Yes."

Whatever he was thinking, she wasn't buying into it. "More stir-fry?"

"To tell you the truth, I can't remember when I ate a proper dinner last. Eating out isn't anyone's idea of eating right." Mark grinned, the leaping flickers of the candle dancing on the fine molding of his jaw, making her want to trace a finger slowly over it.

Nikki prodded the vegetable on her plate with her fork and then took a mouthful.

"But," Mark continued, "that's the price of being a Big Brother."

Nikki nearly choked. "You're a Big Brother?"

"Uh-huh. Some evenings I play basketball with one of the kids. We go to McDonald's after shooting hoops–er, playing basketball."

Nikki stared at him amazed, suddenly hit by a new insight. She thought he had a date the evenings he was out, she hadn't imagined he had an interest in anything besides work. Yet, why did she find it so unbelievable? Wasn't he supposed to be at the fundraiser where Ellen had first told Nikki about the grandson she doted on?

Warmth made her face flush as she savored the thought of Mark in this incredible light. She felt as if she could sit there watching him forever.

"I like to see the kids make something of their lives, at least my 'kid brother.' I never had any of my own brothers or sisters." A faraway look caressed his face. "I missed the fights, the camaraderie, the family outings that kids go through, especially after my mother died. When she became ill, my grandmother stepped in and took care of me."

He put down his fork with a faint tinkle and pushed the plate away.

Nikki went taut with interest. Mark was a walking volume of revelations. It took a power outage to reveal the human side of him.

Whoa! A red flag went up in her head. She wasn't supposed to soften just because he laid open an insight or two about himself, but add in the heart-stopping looks and she shifted in her chair. Nikki didn't want to see Mark as a compassionate, caring man, one who was good with kids. It put impossible dreams in her head, dreams Nikki knew would never come true. She needed the quickest way out of there. The sanctuary of her apartment beckoned like a starving man for a crust of bread. Still, she couldn't just leave with the dishes spread out on the table and the counter cluttered with pans and ladles.

The panic subsided, and she decided to learn more. If she kept him talking, Nikki felt sure she'd find a less altruistic reason for Mark's association with the Big Brother Organization.

Another side of her prodded her to keep him talking. "Does it take a lot out of you, being a Big Brother?" Nikki tried to visualize Mark wearing gray sweats, guarding, trying to make a slam dunk, which he could with his height and athletic build and a little effort.

"Sometimes," Mark said. "My 'kid brother' went through a difficult phase, his grades were dropping like a ton of bricks without concrete reinforcement. That's when I really laid it out, told him he was wasting his life and a good mind. I even tutored him in math and, between his counselor and me, we pulled him out of it. I have to admit he gave me some sleepless nights." His eyes suddenly assumed a glazed, faraway look. "As a reward, I took him to a Bulls game. We dined on dogs and nachos."

"Well, I can't compete with that menu, can I?" Nikki said with a laugh. He still had to compliment her cooking.

Mark got up, picked up his plate, and placed it in the sink. "Are you fishing for compliments on your cooking?" A lopsided grin spread across his face like the Cheshire Cat's smile in *Alice in Wonderland*.

"Of course not." Nikki felt herself flushing at her moment of weakness in saying what she did. The trajectory of their footsteps going back and forth from the counter brought them face to face with each other, forcing her to look up straight into his eyes and seeing an amused look there.

"I was just asking if the cooking was alright," she said,

feeling deflated. Darned if she was angling for a compliment from this unimaginative man who probably couldn't compliment his way out of a circle of leprechauns. He stood in front of her like a basketball player blocking a pass, except his arms weren't raised. He took the dishes from her and placed them on the counter.

"The cooking is fine. And here's a reward for the chef." He tipped her chin up slowly and placed a kiss full on her lips. Slipping his arm around her waist, his mouth brushed hers again, this time more demanding.

Nikki brought the palms of her hands against his chest to push him away, feeling his corded muscles beneath her palms. Then, swept away by the musky scent of his aftershave and his firm grasp, she could resist no longer. Her arms entwined around his neck and she returned his urgent kiss with a matching fervor of her own.

Minutes became an eternity, silent but for the drumbeat of her own heart, or was it the thud of his? She couldn't tell. Enough of this arrant lack of control on her part–whatever he had in mind she didn't have to follow along with him for the ride. Why did she have to fall all to pieces at his firm touch? Nikki struggled out of his arms at last.

"No," she said. "This isn't what I want at all."

Annoyed with herself for losing her composure so easily, she flushed with embarrassment.

"And you," she said, her breath coming in short spurts, "you had no business..." Nikki wiped her mouth with the back of her hand.

Mark took a step away from her, threw back his head, and laughed. "Bet you've been kissed like that before, so why the virginal modesty? Or–have you?"

"Don't be ridiculous," Nikki said, frothing with annoyance

at the charade that just took place, and determined to get to the bottom of it. Neither of them had scripted it, she knew she hadn't. But she couldn't be sure of his motives. "What did you mean by that?"

"What?" Mark's eyes opened wide with feigned innocence. "The kiss? I was just thanking you for a lovely dinner."

He moved to the counter, picked up a glass of water, and drank it slowly, savoring each sip. "You were angling for a compliment on your cooking. I paid you a compliment."

"Are you in the habit of kissing your cooks?"

Humiliation mixed with embarrassment surged within her. He must be from a long line of ancestors who grabbed parlor maids and kissed them behind the stairs, or worse. For a gloomy, memory-loaded second, she remembered a similar incident long ago—something she'd seen. Her father was caught kissing the girl who groomed his polo pony, and it had taken all her will power to block that out of her mind as a child. That was when her father fell off the pedestal she'd put him on.

"Just the beautiful ones," he said, appearing nonchalant, causing her to wince somewhere deep inside.

He returned the glass to the counter. "Seriously, I'm sorry if I caught you unawares, or offended you." His face assumed its usual expression of granite hardness. "That wasn't my intention. I apologize if I overstepped my mark." His tone hardly sounded apologetic.

Nikki gathered the dishes, covered them, and slid them into the refrigerator. As much as she couldn't stand being there, she had her job to finish. Mark's compliment on her cooking, such as it was, was given in an offhand manner at best. Confusion pounded in her head at the thought of that kiss and her own shameless response. She couldn't fathom what had gotten into him.

From the corner of her eye she saw Mark striding back and forth, helping to clear the table. Cold reserve showed in the grim set of his features. He regretted the kiss already, Nikki thought. Why wouldn't he? He'd kissed her almost on a dare in return for her whining remark that he'd never complimented her cooking. Why would he? She was only the hired help.

"You needn't bother with clearing up." His voice, crisp and clear, broke the silence. "I'll take care of it. Now, if you'll excuse me, I have to get to work."

"I'd like to finish the dishes," Nikki said with firmness. She wasn't running away like a frightened little mouse trying to escape a trap.

"Alright," Mark said, "if you insist."

He turned to face her. His expression hadn't changed from the preoccupation that had permanently settled there. "I have to leave earlier than usual tomorrow, so I won't be needing breakfast." He moved toward the kitchen entrance and disappeared into the enveloping darkness of the living room beyond.

Nikki clamped her teeth down on her lower lip and sprinkled detergent in the dishwasher, her mind working furiously. Mark was leaving early for the office tomorrow. Good, she wouldn't have to face him. Did he really have to leave early or was it just a ruse to avoiding running into her?

A sudden weariness dragged her down. What had happened? They had crossed the line between employer and employee. Somehow, under the conditions of the evening that fine line had been obliterated, and now what they had was a fine mess!

Nikki placed the last plate in the dishwasher and shut the

door. The next minute, the lights flicked on and Nikki blinked in the eye-popping brightness, trying to adjust to the white glare. She grimaced. Too bad the lights hadn't come on earlier when she could have served dinner and left. Well, she was leaving now.

She wiped her hands and walked into the foyer through the back door to her apartment, aware of the total silence behind her.

Mark looked up as the lights flooded the study, and he heaved a sigh of extreme relief. At least now he could concentrate on the materials cost projections he was staring at. The bar charts and graphs looked like so many daggers accusing him of abandoning them and all that they stood for. Normally, he'd have no trouble with making sense of these, but tonight the figures seemed to be doing the Dance of the Whirling Dervish in front of his eyes. The only thing he kept seeing in his mind's eye was Nikki–curvaceous, alluring Nikki with that faint lemony perfume she used and the hollow of her throat into which he had the incredible urge to bury his face.

He flicked the papers in his hand with exasperation. What was he doing when he should be jotting down recommendations for the proposed changes? As for why he'd kissed her–he had no satisfactory explanation for that even for himself, except that in the glow of the candlelight, her face and mouth appeared too inviting for him to resist. And when she asked how he liked her cooking, it wasn't her cooking he'd been thinking of.

Mark pushed his swivel chair back and stood up, dragged his fingers through his hair, and paced the room. How was he going to face her tomorrow? And the day after? Just as well he had to meet the guys about cost analysis tomorrow–he could skip breakfast and catch a bite to eat at the office. That way, he'd avoid seeing Nikki. A muscle flicked in his jaw. God, he'd do anything to see her again. He shook his head. Had he gone mad? It was official; he'd gone mad.

Mark returned to his desk. Nikki wasn't saying anything about herself. Sure, she needed the money, but was that all it was? Was she planning on taking Ellen for a further ride? Ellen was known to finance college educations for those with a hard-luck story, and Mark just wasn't sure this wasn't a similar situation.

Ellen wasn't wealthy by any means–just what Mark made sure she had, much to her opposition. She was a proud woman and didn't think much of being financially helped by her adored grandson.

Mark sucked in a deep breath. Well, he knew how to deal with Nikki, and he knew how to keep his distance. He'd had plenty of practice shutting away his feelings, keeping them to himself–that was his way of coping with the scarcity of love he'd experienced after his mother died and his father lost himself in building his architectural empire.

When Dad married Marnie, pretty but self-absorbed Marnie, that clinched the whole thing for Mark. No life but cold, hard work, occasionally dating just to get the chic, slinky women off his back. Could Nikki be just another Marnie? Fear knotted painfully in his throat and he willed it to go away. What did he care what she was like? It was nothing to him. Liar, a little voice nagged. As much as he didn't want to, he did care.

Mark slapped the desk with a flattened palm and looked at the papers in front of him. It wasn't any use. The figures were still dancing on the sheets spread over his desk and they weren't making sense.

Time for a talk with Gran. And, of course, he'd have to make sure he showed only a professional curiosity about Nikki. Gran had hawk eyes and she looked for things she imagined she saw—women-type things. Tomorrow, he'd go to the Institute and surprise her by taking her out to lunch. She always said she never saw enough of him—not eating right, not thinking of settling down—how easily she sneaked that in! Maybe if he spent some time with her, it would put her mind at ease about him.

Mark rolled up his sleeves and took in a bellyful of air. If he could get a word in edgewise, he could slip in a question or two about Nikki. Ha! The ultimate smooth-talking guy with finesse.

The students from the morning session with Signey crowded around, watching goggle-eyed as she dumped a handful of small pieces of paper into a large, dramatic-looking felt hat.

"A drum roll, please..." she said, affecting a deep, menacing tone. One of the students grabbed a thick copper-bottomed pan and beat ominously on it.

"And the winner is...Ellen Carstens." Signey threw her a winning smile. Ellen tossed up her hands in mock despair.

"Me?"

"Yes," Signey replied. "You're the lucky one to do up a meal on short notice. This is a trial run for when a barrage of guests drop in unannounced at your doorstep and you don't have the heart to turn them away or—horrors!—take them to McDonald's. What do you do?"

"Er...call Chinese carry-out?" There was a roar of laughter.

"Well, yes, once in a while, but gourmet cooks don't take

the easy way out."

So Ellen was drafted to cook a special luncheon and invite two people of her choice.

"Need any help with the prepping?" Nikki asked. The chef was allowed to choose his or her "partner in crime" as well.

"Maybe you could help me chop, puree, and sauté. The menu of choice is Ribs of Beef au Vin Rouge." While she started preparing the dish, Ellen explained what she was doing and Nikki handed her the ingredients in the right form.

A delicious mouth-watering aroma filled the sunlight-splattered room, and Nikki took a deep breath. Ellen was a superb cook, but she hid it under an easy-going manner. Nikki smiled to herself. Ellen was so full of surprises, no telling what she'd do next!

Nikki didn't have to wait long to find out. After the ribs were ready and placed in a large, serving dish, class was dismissed. "You and I are the happy partakers of this dish," Ellen said, clearing a small table on one side of the room, which was set up for dining after a demo lesson. "Unless..." Ellen's attention seemed suddenly sidetracked by somebody who stood against the doorway of the room, "I persuade my dear grandson to taste-test my masterpiece."

"Hello, Gran." Mark stood grinning at her, and then his gaze drifted to Nikki and locked with hers. A few moments dragged by–electric moments it seemed to Nikki, as they couldn't break off eye contact. Her face flushed when she remembered his kiss of last night. Was it just last night? It seemed like a lifetime had passed in between her wondering what he was up to and where they stood as employer and employee.

"Wouldn't you know it? I almost forgot," Ellen's voice

suddenly jolted her back to the present like a fire alarm. "The men are coming to deliver my new washing machine and I've got to be there. I suppose the maid could let them in but she doesn't know..." She turned to Nikki, looking distressed. "Would you mind terribly, dear, if I went home, and you and Mark finished off this great spread?" Ellen was already half way out the door, purse in hand.

It took Nikki a few moments to gather her thoughts. She glanced at Mark, who sported a wicked grin on his face. Why was he grinning like that?

"Alright, Gran, dear. If you're sure we're doing you a favor." He kissed her before letting her go.

"Well, here we are again." Mark unfolded his napkin and helped himself to the delicious-looking entree Ellen had prepared. "My grandmother would be miffed if I refused to stay for this sumptuous lunch."

So that was why Mark had decided to stay, to please Ellen, which was understandable because she was such a dear. But then, a twinge of disappointment twisted itself in her mind thinking Mark wouldn't want to have lunch with her and repeat his mistake of last night.

Nikki dished out the beef onto her plate. "So you could be sitting here with anybody. What am I—chopped liver?" Nikki said lightly.

Mark let his gaze linger on her, sliding deliberately over her face, mouth, and neck until Nikki felt herself blushing like an ingénue.

"No, not quite. But you'd be embarrassed if you knew." He flashed a gleaming smile. "Seriously, I'm glad to have delicious female company for lunch today. The alternative is to eat with a bunch of guys in rolled-up shirt sleeves discussing cost projections."

"I don't know in what sense to take your compliment," Nikki said.

Flirting seemed second nature to him. He must have had so many rehearsals that he had it down pat, and women probably hung on his every word. Well, not this one! Still, could she blame them? Her gaze rested on him involuntarily, taking in the casual splendor of his suit, his hair tousled from the breeze outside. His tan had deepened, undoubtedly from being at outdoor construction sites.

"Take it in whatever way you like. You must have your share of compliments from adoring males." He cupped his face in his hand and stared at her.

Men who took you out and then quickly looked for every opportunity to take you upstairs to their apartment were not considered complimentary beings. But she was no fool, either; she knew she had good looks.

"You're right. I've had my share of compliments, but I prefer to take them with a pinch of salt." She looked him right in the eye even though a thud had started in her chest and she wondered if he could hear.

"In other words, I'm just coming on to you and I'd better not waste my time."

"Something like that." A feeling of complacency spread over her. "Besides, what was that you said about my trapping you?"

"Aha, but you forget, if I come on to you, I'm the one that's making the move." A slow, teasing smile lit up Mark's face, driving her utterly crazy.

"You wish. And I'm the one who'll be resisting your move." Nikki tried to keep her voice level. No point in him getting the slightest hint that he was completely dislodging her composure—what jelly-like variety of it she had by now.

"Look. Time's a-wasting and let's not let this great food get cold," Mark said.

They enjoyed the succulent beef and side dish of snap peas in a white sauce, after which Nikki washed and put away the dishes in the cabinet.

"Can I drop you somewhere if you're finished here?" Was it just her feeling or was Mark lingering?

"No, I have my car in the lot."

"I'll walk you to it."

Definitely lingering, she thought.

"My car's in the lot too," Mark said.

That was when Nikki came down to earth with a thud faster than an air balloon without helium, and she knew this was where they parted company.

Nikki walked briskly to the parking lot, got in her car, and started the engine.

"Thank you for an enjoyable lunch," Mark said.

"I didn't make lunch."

"But you provided the company." Another heart-stopping grin accompanied his remark.

"You're welcome," Nikki said and pulled away. How conveniently lucky that Ellen had to leave! Had she planned it that way?

CHAPTER FIVE

"The completed project is going to be state-of-the-art, thanks to the new dimensions and revised cost projections." Dave held his coffee mug aloft and paced the boardroom. "Increasing the cash outlay even marginally will bring in solid returns."

Mark nodded and took a sip of coffee. His mouth was parched and dry from talking all morning to the teams working on the Renaissance Project. No doubt but that the Aqua Fit Gym, Gift Shop, and the Hospitality Lounge all were going to be added attractions to the seniors' condo. The ultimate in retirement living, and Gran would love it!

He hadn't broached the subject of moving her out of that crusty old bungalow of hers into this new place when it was finished. But he would, and soon.

"Wouldn't do to spare any expense when the company is dead set on turning out a superior product," Mark said. "When it's all done, the outside work begins."

"Landscaping?"

Mark nodded. "I've put Ted in charge of that."

"By the way, a few of the older residents we relocated have been asking about Nikki Slater," Dave said. Mark turned around and set his coffee mug down on the table with a thud. "Oh?"

"Seems she was a great help to them–took them shopping,

brought groceries, gave them cooking lessons." Dave threw out the information as if he were announcing the daily weather.

The mention of Nikki set off an uncontrollable pounding in his chest. Could he be wrong about her? Could she be genuinely altruistic, caring about the elderly in general, and Ellen in particular? This new information sandbagged him right between the eyes just when he'd gotten into a state of comfortable skepticism about her.

"What did you say?" Mark asked.

"Nothing. I don't even know where she is." Dave looked as if he was about ready to give up the subject. Still, it would be odd if he came to find out somehow, somewhere, that Nikki worked for Mark.

"Matter of fact, Nikki works for me."

Dave, who was stuffing papers into his briefcase, stopped and turned around. "What? Well, you've been pretty secretive about this, guy!" He looked amused.

"Actually, my grandmother, Ellen, is a friend of hers and she fixed up the job as a housekeeper and cook as a favor to Nikki. And I needed a cook since Mrs. Babbitt left."

All legal and above board, Mark thought. He wouldn't have been in this predicament if he weren't accommodating Nikki–and Ellen, in a way.

"And you can wipe that grin off your face." A growing sense of irritation had him wondering if Dave would leave any time soon.

"Just remembered one of them commented on how pretty she was."

"I'll be sure and tell her between dinner and dessert."

"I just bet you'll do that in your own inimitable way, you sly dog." Dave's grin got wider and he picked up his briefcase. "Off to work."

"A cute housekeeper." Dave walked to the door shaking his head. "What next?"

What next? Mark thought, glancing at his watch. Eleven. He was meeting a client for an early lunch in about half an hour or so.

Dave's tongue-in-cheek comments had jostled him somewhat—not because he couldn't handle them, but because he wondered if there was any truth to them. Deep down, what did he feel about the intriguing woman Nikki was, with just the right touch of mystery in those green eyes shining out of a face that glowed with a pinkish golden tan. Did she even know how mind-boggingly beautiful she was? No. She didn't seem aware of it, while the women he'd dated wasted no opportunity to pat their hair into place or examine their lipstick or preen themselves as they passed a mirror or even a windowpane.

And what her presence did to him! He'd have to hold his raging hormones in check if he didn't want her to know. This morning, for instance...he remembered how she'd walked in with a red ribbon tied loosely through that blazing hair of hers as she put the eggs and toast on the table. He'd wanted to untie it and lead her to the bedroom. It was all he could do to wrap his fingers tightly around his glass of orange juice.

"Are the eggs okay?" she asked, pouring the coffee.

"Sure. Fine." What was *not* okay was what she could do to him without even knowing it. They'd both felt awkward after their lunch together yesterday. He could sense it.

"So what are you cooking at school today?" he asked to break the silence.

"Don't know. The instructor is going to draw it out of a hat." Her dreamy gaze seemed to wash over him in the most tantalizing way, or was he imagining it?

"Isn't that a little inconvenient—not knowing?"

"No. A surprise is good. Life, as in cooking, is full of surprises, so why not be prepared?"

"Aren't you the philosophical one!" On that profound note, he'd left for the office after barely brushing past her in the corridor. He'd been tempted to grab her and crush a kiss on those full lips, but instead he'd said, "Have a nice day."

"How was lunch the other day?" Ellen asked.

They had just finished a harrowing test on soufflés and soups, where each student prepared a presentation to be graded. Ellen, as usual, ranked first with her oyster soup followed by Nikki, a close second, with her ingenious preparation of New England clam chowder.

They were having bag lunches out in the open-air patio. A breeze blew off Lake Michigan, waving the blue and yellow awnings above them. Today, the stickiness was absent, and the air shimmered in blues and greens.

"It was delicious. You're a gourmet cook, Ellen, right up there with the great chefs of Europe." Nikki popped grapes into her mouth and then regretted it–they were nothing but sugar balls. She took her ham sandwich out and started munching on it.

"That's not what I meant, my dear." Ellen cocked her head and waited.

"Aha...I knew you had something up your sleeve." Nikki was pleased with herself for smelling a rat in Ellen's spur-of-the moment invitation to the delectable lunch she'd prepared.

"Why, whatever do you mean?" Ellen's gray eyes widened. "I had nothing in mind when I asked you to lunch, just that it was a pity to let a perfectly good dish go to waste."

"Come on, 'fess up, Ellen," Nikki said, laughing.

"Put it that way, my dear, you can't blame me for trying.

That grandson of mine needs to settle down." Ellen's face brightened with hope.

"That's an admirable sentiment, but I'm not the one." Nikki's words sounded defiant, as if she were denying it to herself.

In the days after that serendipitously arranged lunch, neither Mark not Nikki knew how to behave around each other. For her part, Nikki felt Mark's gaze following her when she wasn't looking, and when she did, she would catch a questioning look in his eyes. Whatever he was thinking when he walked in to have his breakfast or dinner, she didn't want to know. All she wanted was to do her chores and get out of there fast. He seemed to carry an aura about him that was hard to ignore. What was worse, she'd catch an amused glint in his eye now and then.

"Don't move so fast. I'm not an ogre waiting to pounce on you. I just want my breakfast and then I'm off," he said at one point, holding up both his hands in a mock hands-off gesture.

"I'm not worried," Nikki had said. "You're just in my way when I'm trying to set the table." She'd felt like a stupid schoolgirl blushing at the thought of her teenage idol. Goodness sakes, she was a grown woman—couldn't she handle this handsome devil with a smile that would corrupt the gods a little better than this?

"I should really be giving you a kiss before I leave. One for the day, after this breakfast," he said when he was done eating."

"Then you liked the breakfast." She'd brazenly ignored the rest of his remark.

He shrugged. "That was okay. I was referring to the chef with the hair ribbon in her hair.

Nikki rolled her eyes. "The salary you pay me will do

nicely, thank you."

"Too bad." He got up and hefted his briefcase. "The kiss would have made your day."

She watched him stride out the door leaving her somewhere between trembling with annoyance and zooming with unbridled pleasure at his silly remark.

"Nikki?" Ellen's voice landed her squarely back into reality. "My dear, you're off in some other world."

"Sorry. I was just thinking about tomorrow's cooking assignments." And wondering where her attraction to him was leading. Into trouble, no doubt. She'd rather cut out her tongue than let Ellen have any inkling of it. A housekeeper in love with her boss wasn't anyone's idea of an ideal situation.

Ellen's eyes narrowed. "You're sure?"

Nikki raised her right hand. "Girl Scout's honor."

"In that case, let's discuss tomorrow's class. Now I think..." Ellen happily discussed the upcoming event–a visiting chef from Provence, and she was going to take notes.

Nikki heaved an inward sigh of relief not to have to go through a wringer of questions from Ellen, however well meant.

Nikki stacked the plates and the wooden platter that had held the sirloin steak and placed them in the sink.

"You seem to enjoy cooking. I'll give you that." Mark rose from the table. "Need any help with those, or washing up?"

"I can manage, thanks." Nikki suppressed an urge to giggle. She could just see Mark bending over the sink with an apron tied around his middle. Still, he'd asked, and that was a first. And he'd noticed she loved cooking–would wonders never cease!

Rekha Ambardar

Yesterday, he'd come in and made himself a drink before dinner and asked how her day had been. Fine, she'd replied, without going into the details. She wanted to finish her work there and do some necessary shopping for her apartment.

"Do you realize I don't know anything about you?" Mark said suddenly.

Nikki turned around. They were in the living room where she'd come to remove a glass left there when Mark had had a cola. Standing there in the large, brightly lit room wearing jeans and a T-shirt, he looked young–too young to be a successful, world-class architect, and making her pulses throb like wires carrying an electrical charge.

"What could you possibly want to know about me?" She breezed past him carrying the solitary glass, feeling foolish–she could have collected it later.

"About your family, your interests." Mark stood in front of her, blocking her path. "Will you stand still long enough for me to talk to you?"

Nikki looked straight at him. "How interesting can a housekeeper's life be?" She gave a careless laugh, hoping to deflect him from his question, but he wouldn't be distracted.

"You've got a point there." He sounded thoughtful, or was that just a pose? "Do you have family? Sisters and brothers?"

"Parents," Nikki said and started walking to the kitchen. "No siblings. My folks own a business which keeps them busy. I was pretty much on my own. That's about all there is to it."

"*Hmm*. Except you seem to have just a touch of mystery about you."

Nikki's heart thumped. "Why do you say that?"

"You seem so...self-contained."

Nikki laughed in relief. "When you're paying your own

81

way you have to be self-reliant. What's mysterious about that?"

They were in the kitchen where she was letting the dishes soak in warm, sudsy water. She turned from the sink to face him.

Mark's handsome face showed no expression. What was he getting at? "You seem to be on a mission."

"Mission?"

"To find something."

"The only mission I'm on is to set up my catering business."

"I've never met a woman as single-minded as you."

He came closer until she almost heard him breathing. "You seem to know what you want."

Suddenly, his words seemed to have an undertone of a double meaning. From a left-handed compliment they turned into an insinuation of deviousness on her part.

"Is that so hard–knowing what I want? Especially when I work hard for it?" Nikki didn't want to make it sound like a sob story, but she was determined to get her point across in case Mark had the notion that she was just a brat wanting everything she saw.

"Don't get me wrong," he said hurriedly, a shade too quickly, giving her the sense that he must have entertained the idea that she *was* a brat up to something.

The phone shrilled in the living room, and Mark headed reluctantly toward it. He'd have liked to carry on the chit-chat with Nikki a while longer, especially since he had gotten her to talk about herself. But he had had to pull it out of her, ever the mysterious female that she was. His previous experience had been with women who told you their hair color at the drop of a hat–and there went the feminine mystique and a guy's interest in it.

He let out a sigh and grabbed the shrieking cell phone. "Hello," he thundered into it, his mind racing toward tomorrow's meetings and the million things he had to do tonight. "Khalid? How are you?"

Mark grinned, thinking of the last time the prince had been here and the all-but-disastrous evening. He hadn't had time to sift it through his mind, hadn't even wanted to be honest with himself on one or two points about the turn of events.

"I haven't forgotten the excellent evening I had at your place." The prince's precisely accented tone came through the line. "In fact, it was so good that I'm about to sound you out on a proposition for your cook, Miss Nikki."

"A proposition?" Mark tamped down whatever he was feeling at the mention of Nikki—a feeling of possessiveness, something he couldn't fathom.

"I would like to hire Miss Nikki for a month to give cooking lessons to the ladies of the royal family. When I mentioned what a feast I had at your place and that I had this proposition in mind, my brother and his wife urged me to make the arrangements. Visa, passport, travel expenses, and her stay here in Dahram will all be underwritten by our Embassy."

Mark listened, a chuckle rumbling deep in his throat. Now he'd heard everything. His cook and housekeeper was being spirited away with the lure of a dazzling salary and an exotic location. Would Nikki fall for the bait?

Khalid's voice came over the line again. "I know it will be an inconvenience for you for a month. I would, of course, defray the cost of finding a temporary replacement for her."

Mark hesitated. "That's a generous offer, but I'll have to decline. If Nikki takes the offer it's up to her." He took in a sharp breath as if he'd been punched in the gut.

"If you'd ask her and let me know, I could talk to her directly." Khalid, ever the smooth diplomat, obviously didn't want to drive a wedge between Mark and any employee of his.

"Of course," Mark said, getting a grip on himself by now. Talk of a bolt from the blue. His cook was being wooed by a prince–strictly business of course. Or was it?

"I'll let Nikki know and get back to you as soon as possible," he said, and hung up.

Mark heard the distant splashing of water in the kitchen. He would settle the matter here and now; and accept whatever Nikki decided. He couldn't keep her chained to a job, and couldn't be dependent on a household employee–he'd just find a temp; he'd done that before. But he'd have the devil to explain to Gran. "You let her go!" He could almost hear her voice quivering with disbelief at his arrant idiocy.

Mark owed it to Khalid as a friend to at least put the offer to Nikki and leave the ball in her court. He walked thoughtfully to the kitchen. No sounds came from there now. Nikki must be finished with the dishes.

His sneakers scuffed the polished hardwood floor of the corridor as he walked toward the kitchen. He felt a little sheepish that Khalid had praised Nikki's culinary talent and he hadn't. Well, he hadn't verbally, but he knew she was a good cook.

He found Nikki untying her apron, ready to leave. She looked up, her hair mussed and a dot of soap suds on her cheek. A crazy longing to brush it away washed over him.

Nikki looked up.

"I had a call from Prince Khalid."

Mark found himself staring at a pair of long, tanned, well-shaped legs with droplets of water clinging to them. In his mind's eye he pictured her in a bathtub covered with soap suds, her hair tousled. What was the matter with him?

"Yes?" He realized with a jolt that Nikki was waiting, a frown puckering her forehead, while he was still reveling in Fantasy Land.

"Er–Prince Khalid asked me if I would sound you out on an offer. He asked if you would be willing to go to Dahram to hold a cooking demo for the women of the royal family."

Mark watched, fascinated with the way her face lit up, her eyes sparkling like the gemstones women wore to a gala, her mouth forming a surprised "O." The kitchen towel she was holding fell from her hand. "That's very flattering. Nice of him to think of me as a candidate."

"He'd like me to call back with an answer from you without too much delay."

A thump of disappointment pulled somewhere in his chest. He could do nothing if she decided to go, even if it was only for a month, and he'd grown accustomed to her face like the song said in that old movie. Her eyes, her face, the way she tilted her head in concentration when setting the table, her quick footsteps that waited a few seconds before opening the front door.

"I'll have to think it over." Nikki picked up the towel from the floor and put it in a plastic bag.

"Don't wait too long." *Take your time*, the words pounded in his head. *Better yet, decide not to go.* This was a flattering offer for Nikki, a great professional experience to put in her résumé. He'd be crazy if he thought she wouldn't even consider it.

"I'll try not to," she said thoughtfully. So thoughtful that it didn't look good for him. She was going to keep him biting his nails in suspense. Was it just a demo, or was Khalid interested in Nikki? Nah! He couldn't be.

"So, do you think you'll take it up?" Mark said, trying to sound nonchalant.

Nikki shook her head. "I hardly think I can do that. I've set myself a time limit by which to finish cooking school, and I don't want to extend it."

An immense weight lifted off his shoulders, or so it seemed to Mark. He could have picked her up bodily and danced around the room.

"Were you under any obligation to the prince to send me there?" she asked.

"No, not unless you chose to go yourself. The prince usually gets what he wants; I thought you'd decide to go."

"But you'd have to hire a temp while I was gone. And you've had your share of temps, haven't you?" Nikki said, a dimple forming in her cheek.

Mark looked away, uneasy in the knowledge that he had almost decided on her behalf and was about to tell the prince that Nikki couldn't make it. But something had prevented him from being as highhanded as that. He forced himself to look at her. "It's up to you." He sounded abrupt. "You can think it over if you like."

"That won't be necessary. Please let the prince know that, pleased as I am, I can't accept the offer."

She turned to leave for her apartment.

A warm wind smacked her in the face as Nikki headed toward the open-air Farmer's Market. She needed to pick up produce for tomorrow's cooking class—a quick soup and salad ensemble. The remnants of the evening were disappearing, and the breeze played around the shoppers sauntering near brightly lit stalls.

She should have been pleased at the Prince's lucrative

offer. What an item to put in a vitae! An overseas demo at the palace in Dahram, no less! But it just didn't mesh with what she had to accomplish in the short time left to complete school.

Nikki stopped at a stall, picked up tomatoes and cucumbers, and paid for them. Maybe she'd pick up chicken broth for her special cabbage soup–tomorrow's theme was A Healthy Meal for Less.

The pleasant night air had brought more people out than she'd expected to see. Preoccupied with her purchases though she was, a sneaking suspicion entered her mind. Mark seemed a little too eager to lend her culinary services to the prince. Why? Was he trying to get rid of her so she wouldn't be in contact with Ellen?

Nikki bristled at the thought. For all his disarming ways, he had an eye in the back of his head, watching her every move with a smattering of suspicion.

A dull throb made itself felt in her chest and she knew why, even if she wouldn't admit it to herself. She was beginning to feel the stirrings of something for Mark. Was it love? It couldn't be, at least she hoped it wasn't! As much as she reminded herself of the employer-employee thing, she hadn't been able to stop her temples from throbbing, her hair spiking at the back of her neck whenever Mark was near. Worse yet, her stubborn dislike of the highhandedness of her parents because of their wealth had prompted her to be wary of Mark. A rich, spoilt guy who had his pick of women–this was how she had him pegged. Yet, in the short moments when they'd managed to connect, he had seemed almost human. Things just didn't add up.

The cucumbers and tomatoes made a clumsy package in her hand, with her purse dangling on her shoulder like a loose tooth, and the plastic bag containing the produce slipped from her hands. She stooped to pick it up. Straightening up, she took a step backward and collided with somebody.

"Whoa. Steady there!"

She whirled around to face Mark as his arms came up to envelop her to prevent her from wobbling like a broken bicycle wheel. She felt herself leaning against the hard muscle of his chest and pulled back.

"You okay?"

"Yes, thank you." Nikki pushed back her hair. "What are you doing here?"

She was perturbed by her collision with the man who had just invaded her thoughts and the solicitous way in which he steadied her with his firm hold. Where had he sprung from?

It was then that she noticed a boy about thirteen or so grinning at her, a Chicago Bulls cap on backwards and his hands stuck in his jeans pockets.

"Meet Kenny. I'm his Big Brother."

Of course! This was probably the day Mark met with his young friend, the one who had trouble in math among other things.

"This is Nikki, my housekeeper," Mark said to Kenny.

"Hey," Kenny grinned. "You're too young to be a housekeeper."

"So you're the young man Mark is so proud of." Nikki was amused at his guileless remark.

The boy beamed with obvious pleasure.

"I think he's aw-right too." Kenny clapped a high five with Mark.

"We just got done playing tennis." Mark wore shorts and a polo T-shirt, and had sweatbands on his wrists.

"Mark bought me a new racquet. It's awesome."

"We were just going for an ice cream. Would you like to

join us?" Mark asked.

"Well...I..." They obviously looked like such good buddies out for the evening that Nikki had no wish to intrude. Besides, it was bad enough what he did to her pounding insides without prolonging it by staying around. "I really need to get back."

"Aw, come on, Nikki. It'll be cool," Kenny said.

Nikki laughed. "Put that way, how can I refuse?"

"Haagen Dazs sound good?"

They strolled on toward the familiar beige and white sign of the ice cream store, where they made their selections. The guys chose enormous cones with two hefty scoops.

"Just one scoop for me," Nikki said.

Mark stayed to get the orders, while Nikki and Kenny grabbed seats near the window. "So you're the lady who takes care of Mark." Kenny looked at her with something like awe.

"I just do the housework, that's all."

"He said you're a great cook."

Nikki flushed. "That's nice of him."

"And I meant it too." Nikki looked up and saw Mark standing there with the ice cream, which he handed to them with an eyebrow quirked in amusement.

"In that case, thank you," Nikki said.

Kenny munched on his cone, oblivious of her and Mark. It felt as though their booth was surrounded by the power of Mark's personality, something from which she had no escape. How different from her memories of Daddy, who never had time to take her for an ice cream. Nor did her mother, for that matter.

"You should play tennis with us," Kenny said between taking large bites of his ice cream.

"I'm too busy. I take classes–cooking classes," Nikki

explained, seeing, the bewildered look on Kenny's face. Apparently, he didn't think adults had any need for classes.

"Maybe someday I can cook something and have you over, if it's okay with Mark." She glanced at him. All this time, she'd been conscious of him listening quietly while watching her at the same time.

"Would you like that, Kenny?" Mark said.

"Yeah." Kenny's eyes lit up.

Nikki finished her ice cream and got up to leave.

"Will I see you again?" Kenny looked up at her.

"I hope so." Nikki gave him a hug. She didn't know what came over her, she only knew she'd have given her right arm for a few hugs in her life as a child. Besides, there was something endearing about Kenny, grimy face and all.

Back in her apartment, Nikki sorted through the vegetables she'd need for tomorrow, wrapped them in cellophane, and stored them in the refrigerator.

After a refreshing shower, as she sat sipping a tall glass of iced tea, her thoughts strayed to running into Mark and Kenny and a sudden warm feeling stole over her. What she'd just witnessed was a new side of Mark and a very attractive one, something she had never seen in the men she'd known before. Mark had a sense of obligation to those less fortunate than himself. She hadn't missed the zapping charge in the air between them, with Kenny sitting there, a teenage umpire happily unaware of them.

"You made quite an impression on Kenny." Mark loosened his tie and threw it over the briefcase balancing on the coffee table.

Nikki smiled. "He's a sweet kid, full of high spirits."

She had been in the middle of cleaning when Mark walked

in.

"He didn't use to be like that when I first met him. He was withdrawn, refusing to talk to adults, no interest in schoolwork." Mark watched her work with obvious curiosity.

Nikki's dusting grew more vigorous as she moved around the living room, unsettled by his observation of her. Was he watching her as an employer or as a man? Because she couldn't help bristling with awareness of him.

"Must you slap that cushion so hard? What has it ever done to you?" Laughter sparkled in his voice and he stood there, arms folded. He could be watching a slapstick comedy, the way his attention seemed riveted.

"Don't mind me. I'm just finishing up here."

"Don't hurry on my account," he said and took a few steps toward Nikki.

Now she knew she had to finish and get out of there at the speed of lightning. She always seemed to be escaping him, and it told her that something troubled her. It was her feelings about Mark—she'd tried to push them far into the back of her mind, as far as they would go where she could almost ignore them—but it was no use. She had to face the fact that he was occupying her thoughts more than he should.

"I'm in no hurry." Nikki pulled herself together. It would be a disaster if he had the slightest idea of what he did to her, standing there watching her work. It might even slip out that she was really no housekeeper.

"So, how long have you known Kenny?"

"A year and a half. I inquired in a few schools about their Big Brother program and found they were looking for volunteers," Mark said with a cockeyed grin. "At first, he wouldn't speak to me. He was brought up by his mother, who's single and lived in the inner city—not the best environment for a kid growing up. Then she got off welfare and got a decent job. They're a lot better off now."

"Hard to believe. He seems so full of life and happy."

She wondered if Mark had helped them financially as well. A warm feeling tugged at her, thinking of what he might be capable of.

"It took some doing."

Mark's perseverance with Kenny amazed her. It was to his credit that he had been able to bring out the best in the child. Still, she needn't get all teary-eyed at what she had just seen happen.

"By the way," he said. "Today I'm home early to go to my tennis game. It's time I started a daily regimen again."

He picked up his briefcase and looked in the direction of the den. "You can stay and finish up what you need to, now that I won't be around." He threw her a sly grin and strode off.

Mark seemed to gauge her thoughts like radar. As she dusted and wiped to the rhythm of her thoughts, they were coming fast and furious. Mark unsettled her. A few more months and she'd be done with cooking school, then she'd have to look for a business location and an apartment. What if she were to move out and shack up with Jenn? The electric impulses flying around in the air here were getting too numerous and her feelings were confusing her, distracting her from her dream. Besides, where on earth could her attraction to Mark lead to but trouble?

Tomorrow. She'd talk to Jenn tomorrow about moving in with her, and things would be just fine.

CHAPTER SIX

"I'd love to have you stay here, if that's what you want." Jenn placed the plates in the sink after they finished the spaghetti and salad she'd whipped up for them.

Nikki looked around the apartment. It would be a tight squeeze for two people. "I've only got a few more months to complete cooking school, and I'm anxious to open my catering service. I even have a name picked out for it." Nikki got up to clear the table.

Monday was Jenn's day off and she had invited Nikki over for dinner, a welcome change from Nikki's usual merry-go-round of housekeeping chores and prepping for class.

In her eagerness to open her business, Nikki had been scouting around for a place that would allow her to have a front office and a fairly large kitchen in the back for the cooking. She had come up with a few possibilities in the Walking Mall area where there was sizeable pedestrian traffic. She planned to take out ads in the *Tribune*, and could hardly wait to finish her classes before opening her service. If all went well, she would hire a small staff later and hold cooking demos.

"Staying here will allow me to look around," Nikki said. "This place is right smack near where I want to locate my business." She ignored the persistent nudge in her conscience that screamed this was not the sole reason. A housekeeper had no business being attracted to her employer, and if she couldn't keep her feelings under wraps, she should leave the scene.

"Does Mark know?" Jenn said it so suddenly that it hit Nikki like a live wire lying in her path.

"I haven't mentioned anything to him yet. I haven't had time, what with classes and work."

Images came unbidden to her mind, such as the click of the front door opening when she was knee-deep in chores. Was it her crazy imagination, or did Mark come in earlier than usual lately? Once, she'd turned around from cleaning the refrigerator and there he stood at the entrance to the kitchen, his tie slung carelessly around his neck, blue shirt sleeves rolled up to the elbows, and a five o'clock shadow on his handsome face, causing her heart to lurch like mad. She'd straightened up and said, "Well, you're home early." And hated herself for saying that–she sounded just like a wife.

"Tennis game tonight," Mark had said, and disappeared into the other room.

Nikki shook herself from her reverie just in time to see Jenn watch her thoughtfully. "Something's afoot," she said finally. "I can smell it."

"Nothing like that. It's just time to move on, to see about setting up my business. I even know what I'm going to call it."

"Sure you're not running away from something–like Mark?"

"Of course not." Nikki felt herself flushing. "Now why would I do that?" Why indeed? Just because Mark was invading her thoughts more than ever to the extent of how to fix her hair... She wished she could forget that sly voice of conscience taunting her.

"I don't know." Jenn ran soapy water over the dishes. "You tell me."

Jenn had touched a nerve, and Nikki knew it. Could it be

true that she was running away from Mark because she couldn't face up to her true feelings about him, and she didn't want to be hurt? He could do that to her–he belonged to the category of rich, spoiled people that she'd been trying to get away from all her life. Technically, he fit in with them, but deep down she knew he was too much of an individual to be just another wealthy, privileged guy. He cared for Kenny and wasn't above being a mentor to the kid.

Nikki picked up the towel, ready to dry the dishes her friend had finished washing. "You're worrying too much. I'm not running away from anything–Mark or otherwise. I've got my agenda clearly cut out, that's all." An assumed bravado invaded her tone and she eyed Jenn closely to see if she was buying this explanation.

"Okay, if that's what you say. You haven't said much about Mark, so I wondered what he was like."

"He's just my employer. Don't worry about me." Nikki smiled. Phew, she thought–bailed out of that one! Jenn was quick at picking up subtle signs, and she would have had a field day with them, like a dog with a bone.

Nikki drove to her apartment and mulled over the words, "just my employer." She wished it was *all* she felt about Mark, not the electrifying, air-tingling attraction that riveted her attention to him every time he was around.

Last evening, for example, he'd fished papers out of his briefcase and stood bending over the dining room table studying them, while Nikki polished the sideboard. She could swear she heard him hold his breath, as she knew she was, every time he stepped into the room. They hadn't said more than a few cordial words to each other, but she remembered how she'd stepped around him cautiously as if afraid of being zapped by an invisible current.

This is ridiculous, she thought, parking her car in the Tivoli Apartments lot. *I'm not a high school teen reliving the magic of Prom Night.*

Nikki let herself into her apartment and set her purse and keys on the kitchen counter. Her glance fell on a napkin from Haagen Dazs. When she had emptied her purse, it remained in a corner of the kitchen counter. How long ago had it been since Mark, Kenny, and she'd had that ice cream? Only a few weeks, but it seemed like a lifetime. It had felt like being together as a family, even though Kenny was an older kid.

She had promised to cook a meal for Kenny, and she hadn't yet. Maybe they could go on a picnic one weekend afternoon, and she could pack a lunch of fried chicken, corn, and potato salad. Now that fall approached, the leaves were turning color, making everything look golden, and that would be perfect weather for a picnic. Nikki held the napkin in her hand for a moment and then put it back on the counter.

The phone rang with a shrill persistence just as Nikki was debating whether she should take a quick shower. She swung around and grabbed it.

"Nikki Slater?" a cool, female voice said. "I'm the nurse in charge of ER at Blair Hospital. Mr. Runyon has been admitted here with a hairline fracture above his ankle. The orthopedic specialist is setting it in a cast just now." For a moment, Nikki felt herself reeling, her heart thundering like a drum.

"Is he okay?" she blurted out, and then took a deep breath. There was no need to sound frantic... But she was, and that frightened her.

"He's doing fine."

"How did he hurt himself?" Nikki asked.

"Playing tennis. He's right here. Would you like to talk to

96

him?"

"Yes, please."

"Nikki?" Mark's deep voice came over the phone line. "Hope I didn't scare you out of your wits." He chuckled softly.

"What happened?"

"I'd been having an especially good game in the second set, but after I served an ace, I came down hard on my left ankle and twisted it."

Nikki felt herself slacken. Mark sounded okay. "Are they bringing you home, or do you want me to come and get you?"

"Bill, my partner, is going to bring me home. He's been a great help."

"I'm glad you're all right," Nikki said.

Silence reigned for a split second. "Are you?"

The grogginess in his voice assumed a velvety resonance causing Nikki to flush. Even over the phone he had the ability to unsettle her.

"Is there anything you need when you get home?"

"Dinner. I'm starved."

"There's roast chicken," Nikki said. She'd prepared it and the fixings before going to Jenn's.

"Sounds good," Mark said. "Oh, and I'll need help with my shower today–just kidding."

"If you need help, you'll get it. And I'm not kidding."

"Yes, ma'am, Dr. Nikki," he said and hung up.

Relief tanked through her to hear him joke. She'd had her share of emergency room visits when her father suffered a mild heart attack several years ago, and it wasn't a pleasant place. It was to Mark's credit that he sounded cheerful when his ankle probably hurt. She was witnessing a new side to Mark, one she didn't know he had.

Nikki headed for the shower. This way she'd be able to do

whatever needed to be done when Mark got home: there was no telling how long she'd have to remain around to help him.

Nikki took the roaster out of the oven and placed it on the counter, while the vegetables steamed on the stove. Almost ready. Sounds emanating from the hallway made her stop her work and walk toward the door. Mark limped in on crutches, and it took all her will power not to run to him, envelop him in her arms, and whisper soothing words.

A big man walked behind Mark carrying a sports bag and a couple of tennis racquets.

"Just dump them anywhere, Bill," Mark said. "I won't be needing them anytime soon."

"Oh, you'll be back sooner than you think, buddy."

"I'll take them." Nikki picked up the bag and the racquets and put them away in the hall closet.

"I'm sorry you hurt your ankle." Nikki felt awkward. She didn't know what to say, even though it bothered her to see him leaning on crutches, looking like a wounded soldier. It made her want to lay his head on her shoulder, comfort him, run her fingers through his hair.

"You and me both." Mark grinned. "They've given me medication for the pain." He winced slightly, and looked toward the sofa.

"Here, let me help you." Nikki took the crutches from him and let him steer himself, his arm across her shoulder, feeling his weight against her. A tremor ran through her with the realization that his strong body, warm against hers, lent her support rather than the other way around.

"Better," he said, settling on the sofa and raising his leg up onto the cushion.

Nikki put a throw pillow under it, feigning nonchalance.

She'd go crazy if he even guessed how much feeling his taut, muscle-bound body against hers had affected her.

"Dinner is ready. I could serve it here."

"Great idea. How about it, Bill? Stay for dinner?"

"I have to leave. I just wanted to make sure you were okay," Bill said, grinning and looking at Nikki. "Looks like you're in good hands."

"Nikki runs the apartment like clockwork, and now she has an invalid on her hands." This time, a serious look crossed Mark's face, a look Nikki couldn't fathom.

"I'll look in on you later," Bill said, and left.

Nikki glanced at Mark. He was still in his tennis shorts and T-shirt, his face drawn and glistening with perspiration. His attempt at joking might have just been a show; he must really be in some pain

"Can I get you anything?"

"What I'd like is a wash. If you'll wrap a plastic garbage bag on my leg and help me to the bathroom, I'd like to have some sort of a bath. I'm sweaty."

Nikki placed a chair in the tub so he could sit in it and take a bath, then found two plastic bags to wrap tightly around his leg and tape them with duct tape, making the bandage water-resistant. Helping him into the tub, she waited until he seated himself and started to strip off his sweaty T-shirt, then left to find him sweat pants with elastic bottoms.

"I'm leaving your clothes here on the towel rack. Let me know if you need help," Nikki said, returning with his clothes. Mark was sitting in the tub behind the shower door.

"Sure you can handle that?" he said with a wicked gurgle in his voice.

"I can double up as a pretty good nurse, I'll have you know." Nikki willed away the wayward pounding in her chest.

She would have to be in the bathroom holding Mark's clothes while he took a bath, she thought, albeit behind the protective veneer of a frosted shower door. She hadn't counted on things coming to this when she decided to take the job, but then she hadn't dreamed of being attracted to her employer either.

Reassured by the sound of running water, Nikki headed toward the kitchen to set the table for dinner. Maybe she could bring the food to his bedroom, where Mark might be more comfortable. Her thoughts slowed her down—Mark's ankle injury put a new complexion on her plans! He needed someone to help him get around, so that meant she wouldn't be able to move in with Jenn...the ankle would take at least a couple of months to set, she figured.

Nikki carved the roast chicken and placed it on a dish, then ladled out the stuffing and gravy. A feeling of confusion wore her down, unlike anything she'd ever felt before. She didn't mind staying on to help Mark—she'd do that for anyone needing help—but she knew what she was starting to feel for Mark, and it wasn't any distant hero-worship. She didn't want to name the word. What a fix she was in!

She let the faucet run over the roasting pan, chewing thoughtfully on her lower lip. This situation was getting more complicated than she had bargained for, and it was starting to unsettle her. She'd had crushes before, but in comparison to Mark the men were total washouts, what she felt then were anemic versions of the mind-boggling revelation of what the real thing might be. Funny thing was that Mark didn't seem to bend over backwards to impress her, as other men had. He appeared content with himself, with what he was, and what he did—except that there seemed to be a compartment in his life that he didn't open up about.

The phone rang somewhere in the far reaches of the

apartment, and she ran to get it. Ten to one it would be one of Mark's friends calling to commiserate about his injury. She'd just take a message and have Mark call back.

Nikki found the cell phone nestled against the armrest of the sofa, and picked it up.

"Hello?"

"Nikki? This is your mother."

The broad Boston drawl unnerved Nikki, coming as it did from out of the blue. She hadn't talked to her mother in ages...every time she'd called, it seemed her mother had been vacationing or attending charity bazaars. The last time they had talked was when Nikki told her about her job as Mark Runyon's housekeeper, and it had nearly given her mother a knockout punch–George Foreman couldn't have done it better in the ring than when Nikki had told her exactly what she did for a living while going to cooking school. She shuddered to think of that conversation now, but forged ahead anyway.

"Well, Mother. Nice to hear from you, but how did you know I'd be here?"

"I tried your apartment. At this time I gathered you'd be fixing your employer's dinner." She made it a point to emphasize "employer."

"Mother, I can't talk for very long. Mark...Mr. Runyon has hurt himself while playing tennis and needs help getting around. Darned if she would tell her Mark was in the shower and would probably need help getting dressed.

"I can't understand you, Nicole." Mrs. Slater used the formal version of Nikki's name to register disapproval. "Instead of working for Mark Runyon, you should be marrying him."

"Mother, things just don't work that way." Nikki wondered how to wriggle out of the conversation without being disrespectful. If only her mother didn't have a one-track mind geared solely to marrying money to keep it in the family, raising babies, and doing charity work as a token gesture. "It might have been okay for you, but I have my plans laid out."

"To be a cook." Her mother's voice sizzled with disdain. "I was hoping I could talk you out of this nonsense, but I see you're going to be stubborn about it, so I won't waste my breath. Since you're in such a hurry, I'll let you go." She hung up in a huff.

Uh-oh, Nikki thought, placing the telephone on the coffee table. She'd have to call her mother back and calm her down, but not today; she was too busy.

It was all quiet in the bathroom. She knocked and opened the door a little. "Are you okay in there? Need any help?'

"Just fine," Mark said. "You can help me out of here. And don't worry, I'm decent–clotheswise anyway."

Nikki didn't know what to expect. Mark had pulled aside the shower door and sat on the chair with the towel underneath him, fully dressed.

"How did you manage to get dressed?" Nikki said.

"Just pulled the clothes off the towel rack. I have a long reach. Helps with playing tennis, too," he said with a grin.

"How do you feel?"

"My ankle feels stiff, but other than that I'm okay. They've given me a strong painkiller for today." Mark edged forward in the chair and pulled his feet out of the tub one by one.

Nikki leaned toward him and helped him out, then slowly walked with him, his arm around her shoulder, to the bedroom where he propelled himself onto the bed.

"Okay?"

He nodded. "Thank you, Nikki. You've been a great

help."

"Wait. Dinner's ready, and you must be starved. Shall I bring it in here?"

"Yes, please."

Nikki went back into the kitchen and arranged a tray with food, a napkin, and a glass of water, then returned to the bedroom.

Mark had propped up his pillows and made himself comfortable. He took the tray from Nikki and said," That looks sumptuous."

"Enjoy your dinner. I'm heading back to clean up," Nikki said. Back in the kitchen, she got busy washing the pans in the sink and putting them away.

Her chores done, Nikki wiped her hands on a hand towel and leaned against the sink. An invisible hand prodded at her to return to Mark, just in case he needed something, but she couldn't yet. She needed time to get her own feelings in focus. She'd indulged herself in the notion that she'd be on her own, and moved out of here, out of Mark's unsettling presence, but now she couldn't. It would be nothing short of ingratitude to Ellen and, in a sense, to Mark as her employer, if she decamped now just to guard her feelings and her slowly melting heart. Seeing Mark in this vulnerable state did something to her, pulled out all the stops on her self-control.

Nikki had been hurt a few times in the past by men whom she thought sincere, opening up all the feelings her giving nature was capable of. But she'd been wrong–time and again–until she swore never again to fall to pieces over a man.

She wrenched the towel from her fingers and threw it on the counter. She'd fallen apart over men less personable than Mark, so what protection did she have against a man as incredible and as mystifying as Mark?

Nikki pushed back a wisp of hair from her forehead and went back to the bedroom. Mark looked up when she entered. "Good dinner."

"You know, it's the first time I've heard you say that." There she went, sounding like a wife again—how disgusting!

"When you're sick or injured, you slow down and notice things, didn't you know?" He took a gulp of water.

"I'm glad you liked it," Nikki said, pleased by the compliment to her cooking even if it had come late. She'd hoped to hear validation of her culinary talents much earlier, had looked for it from Mark, but it had never come. This made up for his earlier lack, and it warmed Nikki. She felt herself glow with pleasure. "I'll off-load the tray and then you can get to sleep."

"I could use the shut eye. I feel all dragged out and done in." Mark lay back on the pillows, wincing a little. "Thank you for all your help."

"Of course," Nikki said in a cool voice. "That's what I'm here for, isn't it?" Now why did she have to put it like that?

He didn't reply for a moment.

"Good night," he said finally. Nikki left the room carrying the tray.

Mark raised his leg onto the sofa and leaned back against the thick cushion with an exasperated groan. On a portable wooden table next to him lay a stack of reports, photos, and cost outlays on the Renaissance Project. Everything was going according to their timeline projections, and yet he found himself brimming with discontentment.

For over two weeks now, he'd been on his back or hobbling around on crutches, having office work sent over to the apartment, and holding team meetings in his PJs, much to the amusement of the company's personnel.

"Think of it as a vacation where you work at home...flex time," they said with a snicker, which he had been too quick to miss.

"Easy for you to say when you can go where you want, when you want," he'd replied, glaring at them.

"You're not doing too badly, with a snazzy housekeeper like Nikki," Dave said, picking up his papers to leave after the meeting. He gave Mark a sly wink.

"All right, go on, have your fun," Mark said. "See what you'd do if you were in my shoes." PJs, to be exact, he thought.

"I'll think about that." Dave grinned like a leprechaun. "You poor baby." Obviously, he couldn't resist that parting shot as he opened the door and shut it after him. Mark shook his head and grinned to himself. Now that he'd seen the progress report on the project and the team had left, he felt better.

He had behaved like a bear this morning when Nikki laid the table for breakfast and he couldn't get on his crutches to hobble around to find his notes for the day's briefing to the team. At one point, he had hopped on one foot and bumped against the leg of the dining table, letting out a yelp–not so much in pain as in disgust and impatience.

"Gad! Who put this table here?" he'd roared.

"It's always been there. Remember?" Nikki smiled at him sweetly. "I could serve breakfast in the kitchen; but it's full of smoke from frying bacon and eggs."

He'd mumbled to himself and jammed his rear end into the chair. The breakfast tasted delicious, he had to admit, but he was in too much of a bad mood to say so. She'd stood there for a moment, obviously waiting to hear if the food was okay, but some perverse goblin in him wouldn't give her that satisfaction. Finally, she'd gone into the kitchen to wash up, and that was that.

Mark, my boy, you hate her seeing you in this helpless condition, that's what your problem is, he thought. He couldn't find excuses to make her stay and chat without seeming to need a hand with the most ordinary things.

The last time he was out with her, if he could call it that, was when he had taken her and Kenny for ice cream. It felt odd...and somehow right in some strange way–her, Kenny, and himself. Was this how families went out together? He hardly remembered, except for vague, episodic memories of his mother taking him out with Gran sometimes. This felt like that transient time in his life. How brief it was!

He remembered at one point Nikki's gaze locking into his, and he hadn't wanted to take his eyes off the luscious curve of her cheek or the way her lashes fanned out like a silky veil. Damn, he was thinking corny thoughts again.

He let out an impatient grunt and, gathering up his papers, shoved them into his briefcase. Right. He was going to get his act in gear–his personal life, not his office work–and he was going to stop moping around without actually knowing why. Could be his sedentary situation, it cramped his style. For one thing, it put a total clamp on dates. If he remembered right, the doctor said he'd be holed up for two months, maybe more.

Mark hobbled to his study and looked around as he made slow progress. These days, Nikki left a little later than usual, making sure he had everything he needed to get him through the day. She walked past him now, carrying a dry-cleaned suit in its plastic bag. God knows he wouldn't need that for a while, and the thought drove him crazy.

"Anything I can get for you?" she said as she hurried by.

"Of course not, I just have a fracture. I'm not dying," he exploded.

"Just asking." She looked miffed as she stopped briefly. Serve him right if she left notes for him and refused to speak to him anymore.

Mark felt himself go hot with annoyance at himself for not having more self control than this. And the reason for his lack of it was standing there right in front of him, looking as delicious as ever in a black skirt and a tight blue T-shirt, her hair bunched up in a knot over her head but leaving tantalizing tendrils over the nape of her neck—which he had the crazy urge to kiss. He even felt the hair on his forearm standing to attention.

"I'm sorry," he said, waving his hand in an *I-give-up* gesture. "If you're done here, I'll see you later. Thanks for setting up before the guys get here for the meeting." Why she bothered when he snapped her head off at every turn he didn't know, but since he'd broken his ankle, Nikki had shown extraordinary patience.

He turned away so he didn't have to watch her swaying toward the bedroom with his suit, hobbled over to the coffee pot set up in the dining room, and poured himself another shot of caffeine. He waited for Nikki to emerge from the bedroom before heading there with his coffee to lick his wounds. Going into the bedroom, he propped himself up on the pillows and drowned himself in the black, liquid depths of the strongly brewed drink.

He'd made a colossal fool of himself by not behaving in a civilized manner despite his annoying foot condition and limited mobility. After all, that wasn't Nikki's fault. If anything, she'd been a great help—or she could be if he didn't have the overwhelming urge to get his hands on her. What was the matter with him? He was behaving like a teen with raging hormones. In high school he'd had moonstruck buddies who'd try to catch the attention of some attractive female teacher, and here he was acting in the same besotted way. He just hoped, for his own sake, that Nikki didn't get wind of what was going on in his mind.

Well, he wasn't going to sit at home much longer. He'd pull on a pair of sweat pants and have somebody drive him to the office, where he could be more hands-on. He wanted to jump into the development of the end product if he had to walk on crutches all the way to the office building.

Having made that decision, he sat back and finished the last of his coffee. The ringing of the bedside phone jolted him, and he reached for it.

"Hello? Oh, hi, Kyle."

It was his old school buddy, with whom he'd played pranks on other kids. Their careers had taken them in different directions, but they still met occasionally to swap anecdotes over a beer. "Haven't heard from you in a while, not since I met your new girlfriend."

"That's what I'm calling you about, buddy. We're getting married and I want you to be best man," Kyle said. The guy sounded excited and it caused an unexpected turmoil somewhere in Mark's gut. It *couldn't* be roiling envy...could it?

"You're kidding! Never thought you'd make up your mind so soon. Last I remember, you were trying to decide between Kara and Sue." Mark couldn't help the sly dig.

"Sue's the only one for me," Kyle said, sounding dreamy and making Mark want to chuckle. "When you meet the right girl..." Kyle's voice trailed away. He had it bad.

There it was, that gut-wrenching envy again. It wasn't like Mark to be anywhere in that vicinity–he had all the knockout dates and women he wanted.

"What's that you say?" Kyle kidded.

"You deserve the best, pal," Mark said, genuinely happy for his childhood partner in pranks. "Thanks for the offer to be best man. But I'm on crutches these days."

"What happened?" Kyle asked, concern rising in his voice.

"Hurt my ankle playing tennis. When's the wedding?"

"In a month."

"Better off getting somebody else. Thanks, though, pal." Mark felt honored that Kyle had him pegged for best man on his special day, but as things stood...

After a few minutes of chit-chat, Mark hung up. The truth was, he didn't really feel like reminiscing about old times and, happy though he was for Kyle, he was reminded that he lacked a certain something in his own life. Squiring a different foxy lady around town each day of the week wasn't exactly conducive to a happy love life. Actually, that wasn't even his particular style—who was he kidding?

Mark hobbled to the bathroom to conduct his morning bath routine. He'd gotten used to tying the plastic bag around his leg and, propelling himself onto the chair in the tub, let the water run over him. God, it felt good! Things he'd taken for granted would have been harder those first few days if it hadn't been for Nikki.

Half an hour later, he sat on the bed splashing aftershave on his face and neck, then pulled on a loose T-shirt and sweat pants. Comfortable at last, he sat on the large soft leather chair in one corner of the room and leafed through his work calendar for the day. He had a conference call with a Far East client who wanted quotes on a project—Lois would put the call through later in the morning—and he also had to check on the vendors' equipment for the Renaissance Project. It wouldn't be long before the building would be ready, and Gran could move into a spanking new place.

He couldn't wait to see her face when he told her, but then a sense of unease rippled across his back and Mark shifted in his chair. It was for her own good, so why did he have these feelings of impending doom?

CHAPTER SEVEN

"It's not that bad, Gran."

Mark leaned back and did leg exercises while seated on the sofa. "I've had this cast on for a few weeks now and the doctor says the bones are knitting well. So it won't be long."

Silence reigned for some moments at the other end. Mark knew his grandmother was envisioning a worst-case scenario for him, a hopeless, dire situation.

Gran would feel better if he had a wife to look after him. She didn't believe he was capable of taking care of himself; after all, she was the one who had sent him a housekeeper and she had old-fashioned ideas about a guy being able to find himself a square meal and match his socks after the drying cycle.

"I'm so worried about you, Mark, dear," she finally admitted. "Now if you'd find a nice girl and settle down..." Her voice trailed off.

"Gran, don't worry so much." As much as he loved her, he had mixed feelings about her constant concern.

"It couldn't be easy limping around." She sounded preoccupied and a tinge morose.

"Now, you know I can't just pick a woman off the street." Mark grinned at Ellen's simple logic about finding a "nice girl," which made sense but was difficult to execute. "If I meet someone I like, I'll be sure to settle down–white picket fence, roses, the whole bit."

"You're just teasing an old woman. Be serious for once."

"Oh, I am."

"Is Nikki taking good care of you?"

Mark suspected she'd been raring to slip in a question about Nikki.

"Yes, she is."

"Now there's a gem of a girl."

"I agree. She'll make some guy a dynamite wife."

First Kyle and then Ellen, with her oblique questions about Nikki, had him chasing wild thoughts about his luscious housekeeper. Not only that, she seemed level-headed and independent in the way she went about her business. And she was completely disinterested in him. Now *that* bruised his ego not a little.

"I'm glad you give credit where it is due and appreciate Nikki's help, especially now," Gran said.

Especially now that he was dependent on her, thought Mark. He let out an involuntary sigh. Each time she came close to navigate him toward his study or the living room, he could feel her body against him. Soft and yielding, it was all he could do not to pull her toward him and plant a long kiss on that mouth of hers. Once or twice she'd looked puzzled when he appeared brusque, but he had to be to save himself from looking like a complete fool. He quit the leg exercises, tucked a pillow under his head, and rested his leg on another. It was late afternoon, and she would be coming in to fix dinner soon.

"Don't worry, Gran, I'm eating right. In fact, Nikki should be along any minute to cook and see if I need anything."

He'd graduated from pajamas to sweats, and sometimes to shorts and a tennis sweater. His ankle didn't ache anymore, just felt stiff. But that, the doctor said, would go away. His work had come by messenger today, and he studied figures and designs until his eyes popped out, so now he'd earned his reward, which would be getting an eyeful of Nikki walking around the apartment with the cleaning caddy, doing the chores.

"I'm glad, dear. I'm off to a Women's Auxiliary meeting."

"Take care of yourself," Mark said and hung up.

He chuckled to himself. He and Ellen were both intense people and workaholics in their own way, reminding each other not to work too hard.

The door leading to the foyer clicked opened and Nikki came in wearing blue jeans and a simple white sleeveless blouse, looking very young. Her hair was tousled and fell in curls around her face. She looked hot and sweaty. Odd, because the days were getting shorter and cooler.

"Busy day?" He realized he sounded like a guy greeting his wife as she came home from a long day at work.

"I'll say. I had to run around looking for ingredients for the out-of-the-hat recipe they handed me to prepare." She swiped the back of her hand across her forehead and then blew away a wisp of hair from her face.

Some demon drove him on in his curious quest to know this detached ice maiden. Did she have a heart that beat as wildly as his did when she appeared through that door, a veritable gold mine of personality and sex appeal? Not one of the women he'd known before was even a patch on her collectively.

"Figures," Mark said and stood up. He used only one crutch now and didn't really need it. "You've been doing your chores and hurrying out of here as if you didn't want to talk to me." He knew he sounded like a bear growling when disturbed from cozy hibernation.

"Well, excuse me." She stood perilously close to him and a faint whiff of some musky perfume played around his nostrils. "I was only going about my business." A puzzled expression flashed through those long, green eyes.

He wanted to stare at her face open-mouthed, but he shook himself free of the urge. "What are you cooking today?"

"Roast duck," Nikki said with a smile. "Something different from your usual fat-free fare."

He turned away. He could just see himself seated in the midst of a sumptuous dinner, with silverware and the strains of a jazz quartet on CD, trying to polish off a duck. He'd been bored of having no one to talk to all day, except the guys on the conference call. Being hemmed in all day corroded a guy's sense of well-being, and the rest of the evening promised no better—he had to e-mail new structural designs to a client in Houston.

Mark threw Nikki a casual glance, trying to conceal the brainwave he just had. "It's too much for me to finish. If you're not doing anything after this, why not join me for dinner?" A feeling of victory jostled him as Nikki looked up at him, her eyes widened, drawing him in with their electrifying magnificence. He'd forced her attention. God, she was a delectable dish!

"I have to get back to see to a few things in my apartment," she began hesitantly. It was a good sign she was considering his offer. It had been a lifetime ago that they'd eaten together.

"You have to eat sometime," Mark said. He'd better give her a little push before she declined altogether. "Besides, I'd like the company. I've been cooped up in here for too long."

"You poor thing." The tease in her voice was unmistakable.

Nikki let her gaze wander over his lean, finely chiseled features, overcome by a mad urge to trail her finger over them. But she took a step away from him. She didn't want him to guess what she felt for him, and against her principles, too. Besides that, she knew exactly how it would seem to him if he had the faintest clue of her attraction to him. He would think that she was trying to trap him into marrying her to leap out of her social class. Nothing could be further from the truth. She turned away to suppress an urge to giggle. How did she get into this predicament?

"Put that way, how can I refuse?" she said, coolly banishing the hammering in her chest. An evening with Mark!

She glanced covertly at him. He looked like one of those handsome Greek statues, dashing in anything he wore. Today it was shorts and a white sweater with blue and red ribbing along the collar and cuffs. He could easily pass for an actor playing a tennis pro.

Her heart sank. He had no right to be this attractive while she had to be in contact with him every day. She had a goal to achieve, and this heart-throbbing impediment was in the way.

"Excuse me while I get dinner ready."

"I can help, you know," Mark said. "Have you noticed how much my limping has improved? Won't be long before the cast comes off."

And he'd be up to his old activities again, of taking out sleek women like Lauren, Nikki thought. Well, maybe that wasn't quite true. He did a lot besides just dating; it was only her jealousy acting up. The thought cast a pall over her mood as she placed the duck, ready for roasting, in the oven. Why did she care? There was nothing whatever between them, except one kiss. Every time they happened to be together, an invisible magnet seemed to pull them closer, yet no words had been spoken about the electricity springing up between them.

"Let's start things off the proper way—some wine first," Mark said after Nikki finished up in the kitchen and while they waited for the duck to cook.

"Don't forget, I'm on duty," she said.

"I won't tell anyone if you don't," Mark replied with a twinkle sparking in his eyes. "Besides, you're not a police officer on a case."

"It's a small duck, but it's going to take a little time. Maybe I'll have some."

Mark took out two crystal wine glasses from the sideboard and poured red wine from the decanter, also fine crystal.

"I promised Kenny a home-cooked meal and haven't done it yet. I've been so busy."

"I miss seeing the guy. No basketball for a while," Mark said, a thoughtful look slowly stealing over his face. "I've been thinking of having him picked up and dropped here in the company car, I just didn't get around to it."

A warmth surged within Nikki. Sweet. He must love that kid.

"You miss him, don't you?"

Mark nodded. "He's like the kid brother I never had."

"You'll have a son of your own, someday," Nikki said, and then regretted it. It seemed intrusive, yet she remembered the look of total and sublime contentment when he kidded and teased Kenny during their ice cream outing.

A tinge of amusement flitted across his face with lightning speed. "It's been known to happen when you find the right person." He grinned. Nikki felt herself go red with embarrassment—what foolishness had made her say that?

"What about you?" He held her by the elbow and gently steered her toward the living room. "What do you see in your future besides catering?"

It came so suddenly that Nikki stopped in her tracks and turned around to face him, steadying her hand to prevent the wine from spilling.

"Are you really interested?"

"Try me."

"All right then." Nikki sat on the sofa and placed her glass on the coffee table. She watched him sit an arm's distance from her, his left arm thrown across the back of the sofa. "I have the usual dreams of settling down with a decent man who respects what I do. Children, someday."

She spoke the words nonchalantly. It had been ages since she'd stopped to think of such things. The only men she'd seen of late were the students at the Institute on a quest for a career like herself. They weren't husband material, and besides that, she wasn't even looking–until a wonder like Mark appeared and made her lose all rationality.

Nikki tried to focus on her glass as she lifted it from the polished coffee table. She felt his questioning look, making her self-conscious. She had revealed too much about herself, but she'd fix that soon enough.

She looked at her watch. "Look at the time! I still have the vegetables to prepare–cauliflower and broccoli in a special sauce, and homemade rolls."

"That can wait until the roast is ready," Mark said firmly. "So relax."

Nikki turned toward him, surprised. He meant what he said; it looked as if he really wanted to sit and talk to her.

"Do you like this sort of work?" He settled back into the sofa, appearing quite content to sit there forever if he chose.

"It might not be my first choice, but, yes, I like it. Besides, it helps me pay my way through school."

"Nothing wrong with that, as long as you're doing good work."

"And am I?'

"What?"

"Doing good work?" A flurry of butterflies started cavorting in her stomach. She hated having to ask; it made her feel so *needy*.

"Yes, I'll admit that."

"You value compliments so much that you don't part with them easily."

Mark threw back his head and guffawed. "Now where did you get the notion that I'm a thankless monster. I'm not, I assure you."

He picked up his glass, pondered it for a while, and took a sip. "It's just that you're an eternal mystery."

"You're mistaken about that. I'm an average working girl."

"Average? No, I don't think so. You're anything but."

Nikki felt her throat tighten with apprehension. "Just what do you mean? Certainly I'm not rich and idle."

"Would you say being rich and idle go hand in hand?"

"The rich seem to have a feeling of entitlement." She knew what she was talking about. Her parents had always expected their position and money to get them noticed and respected. She loved them despite that, but it was a distant sort of love, not the warm, cuddly kind. She felt a sigh coming on and squelched it. "They think a few charities here and there will do them the trick of being pillars of society." There was bitterness in her tone.

"Whoa! Aren't you being a little harsh? Especially when you don't know them. Now, come on, how would you know?"

Nikki took a quick look at him to see if he was being

facetious. No, he was perfectly serious, goading her on, needling her.

"I've been in a position to observe them." Keep it short and simple, she told herself. No sense in getting him curious.

"From the vantage point of your work?" Interest glistened in his eyes as he leaned forward, as if he'd like to know more.

"You might say that."

He paused for a moment. "I see a smattering of prejudice,"

Was she that transparent? Yes, she was prejudiced, but that was because she'd lived that life and hated it. To her passionate way of thinking it seemed hollow, completely without feeling or compassion for one's fellow beings. But then, here was this epitome of the champion of the underprivileged sitting next to her, making a fantastic lie of her prejudices. The only way out of that trap was to find out more about Mark.

"Take yourself, for example." Nikki warmed to her subject. But it was a losing battle for her to keep focused on the topic at hand. He was sitting less than an arm's distance from her, and she could swear she felt his fresh, minty breath. Nikki inched away, trying to be as unobtrusive about it as possible. "You've probably had it all on the proverbial silver platter."

"I don't know if by 'silver platter' you mean the everyday things that make life easy." His mellifluous voice melted over her like butter with its sensual timbre, "but I never took any of that for granted. After I lost my mother I realized how fragile life was."

His words stunned her. He had kept his feelings so hidden that all she'd seen was the suave, debonair exterior. But this showed her another side of Mark, one that wasn't the carefree playboy she thought him.

"I'm sorry." A sudden wave of longing flooded through her. How often had she wished to spend an evening in meaningful conversation with her parents? Their complete absorption in themselves didn't leave room for anyone else in their lives.

The last time she was home, she remembered having a maddening urge to run to them and give them a hug before leaving—anything to make them see her and know she was there. Instead, she'd said goodbye to her mother and father and left, tears coursing down her face as she ran to her car.

Mark shrugged. "I made sure I worked hard, partly so my father would be proud of me."

"And was he?"

"Was he what?"

"Proud of you?"

"He seemed to be." Mark blew out a breath, remembering feeling the power of the Runyon family name, but empty otherwise. "Growing up, I would have liked to have known kids of my own age whom I could bring home to meet my father. I was proud of him. But there was no closeness of the kind a kid dreams of having with his father. We never went fishing, or shared hobbies. All he ever talked about was business and family responsibility." A line dented his forehead. "When I met the inner city kids, I saw that, like me, they had only one parent. The only thing different was that I was affluent and they were poor."

"Like Kenny."

Mark smiled and nodded. "Once a kid I was helping tried to steal my wallet, but I caught him just in time."

"To punish him?"

"No, to save him from himself. I might have done the

same thing in his situation. So, no, I don't take any of this for granted."

Nikki didn't know what to say. Mark was a walking revelation of surprises, unfolding like a late-blooming morning glory and dispatching her preconceived notions of how a guy in Mark's situation would behave.

"And I owe it all to my grandmother for keeping me properly reined in." He grinned. "I'm pretty sure that's what my mother would have wanted."

"You're lucky," Nikki said with a tinge of wistfulness, "you had your mother and Ellen to give you the love a child needs." She tossed out the words lightly, as if she didn't care.

"Something tells me you weren't that lucky." Mark arched an eyebrow. "Am I right?"

Nikki shrugged. "Yes and no. My parents were too far away to care too much about me."

They were, in the emotional sense, she reasoned to herself, so she wasn't lying.

"For all that, you didn't do too badly." Mark looked at her in a way that sent delicious shivers down the small of her back.

He leaned forward and moved away a wisp of hair from her face with his finger. "Sometimes I feel I've known you for a long time. Now why is that, do you suppose?"

His hand tangled through her hair and he pulled her close. In one forward movement she was drawn into the cradle of his arms, his breath warm and moist against her face while her heart raced.

"Nikki, you know as well as I do what's happening to us." His mouth closed over hers for a long, passion-filled moment that took her breath away. Her hands moved up to his hair, feeling its springy thickness under her fingers. She had no desire to back out of his embrace, but calm reason told her that's what she had to do. She wriggled out of his arms.

"No," she said. "This doesn't seem right. Don't you see?"

Mark pulled back, a thin line appearing on his forehead. "See what? What do you mean?" he asked, spacing the words evenly.

"You've been cooped up for so long and I'm the only female you've seen in all that time."

She didn't think it was her incredible allure that turned him on. She'd have liked to think that, but he had been quarantined for so long that anything in a skirt would have seemed attractive to him. It could have been anyone instead of her, and he'd behave in exactly the same way.

"Oh, I see. You think it's the old story of the starving male out to lasso the first woman he can find. Can you really believe that of me? When have I ever given you that impression? I've never treated you with anything but respect, and if it is because of the kiss, then who are you to put on the 'maiden aunt' act? You know you liked it too, you were with me every step of the way. I wasn't born yesterday." His voice dripped with hurt; he rifled his fingers through his hair in an impatient motion and then got up to sit in the armchair.

"No thanks, I can get around by myself," he said stiffly, seeing her get up to help him. "Don't trouble yourself on my account."

Nikki shrank from the hardness in his tone; it sent a chill through her. Her spirits dropped lower than a barometer reading in an ice storm. Why couldn't she have let things go on as they were, both of them sitting on the sofa? After all, she was enjoying it, swept along with the intensity of her attraction to him. But the honest side of her wouldn't let it go on. She had to question his motives and, most of all, her own. Did she really want to be caught in a situation that was no more than a charade for both of them? Her wondering if any woman would do for him, given his vulnerable situation. As for Mark–why would he find his housekeeper so wildly attractive that he'd make a pass at her?

"It's time I checked on dinner," Nikki said, desperately wanting get away from his dangerous charm, and what better reason than to see about the roast and the fixings? "If you'll excuse me, I'll take the glasses back."

She picked up the half-empty wine glasses to take back to the kitchen.

"Sure, go ahead. Don't let me stop you. I'll be in the den." He faced her, his gaze stopping her in a long, hypnotic hold. "Running away as usual, aren't you?" He ripped out the words impatiently.

"Of course not. I have chores to see to." She'd never been in a situation like this. All she knew was that she had to get away fast to be able to think clearly, and being surrounded by all that male magnetism didn't allow her to have one rational thought in her head.

Nikki walked away, hoping she appeared cool and in command of herself. She wished now she hadn't agreed to stay for dinner. If she hadn't, she'd be in her apartment cooling off and thinking calmly of how to deal with Mark.

The aroma of delicately seasoned potatoes and vegetables sautéing filled the kitchen as Nikki worked to a symphony of total silence in the rest of the apartment. What was Mark doing in the den? Was he looking at plans, designs, or whatever occupied his time these days? An uneasy feeling nudged her at the thought of sitting through an awkward dinner with him.

Ready at last, Nikki set the kitchen table. Mark didn't want to be served at the sweeping dining room table that smacked of formal evening entertaining. That was food for thought...his tastes were surprisingly simple.

Nikki walked over to the den and peeked in. He was standing, leaning on one crutch and bent over sheaves of papers on the drafting table.

"Dinner's ready."

He looked up. "Good, I'm starved."

He sounded as if the last hour or so hadn't taken place at all. Whatever he was working on had engaged his attention altogether, which was a good sign. He might be in a better mood, but that still didn't help her predicament.

She needn't have worried about awkwardness at dinnertime. Mark helped himself to the food like a man who hadn't eaten the whole day, even though he'd made himself a good lunch out of the corned beef she'd prepared and left in the refrigerator.

"This is not bad," he said, tucking into the roast duck and potatoes. "By the way, you'd be interested to know the seniors' condo is almost completed. It won't be long before the residents can move in." He laid his fork down and looked at her. "Ellen should be able to move into a new apartment very soon."

Nikki looked up suddenly. "I didn't know Ellen wanted to move."

"She doesn't know it yet, but this is the best place for her," Mark said.

Nikki noticed a tone of complacency in his voice that she didn't recognize.

"How do you know that? After all, she's lived in her present house for many years."

To her knowledge, Ellen loved her old house. Nikki had never been there, but Ellen spoke of it with pride and sometimes with poignancy. It was more than a structure; to

Ellen, her house was a living thing, something she'd cherished for a lifetime, nurtured by memories.

"That house is too old for her. This way, she'll meet other people and she won't be by herself."

"Aren't you being a little heavy-handed about this? Making a decision for her?"

"Wait a minute," Mark said, looking up sharply. "It's for her own good."

"What makes you think she wouldn't know her own mind about this?" Nikki felt a surge of irritability and disbelief.

"Are you telling me I don't know my own grandmother or what's good for her?" The coldness in his voice returned and spilled out. "Because if you are you're wasting your time."

His words riled her all the more because she cared about Ellen as a dear friend. He couldn't assume that concern for Ellen was off limits to her just because she was no blood relative of the older woman.

Nikki stared at him, defiance welling up within her. "Ellen may be your grandmother, but she's my friend and a dear one. For a woman her age, the home she brought up her children in means a lot," Nikki said. "Yanking her out of it to settle her in a brand new condominium would be a radical change in her lifestyle." She spoke with quiet firmness, making Mark look at her as if he were seeing her for the first time–but only for a moment.

"Would I yank her out of her home if I thought it would cause her unhappiness?" he said.

"Obviously we have different ideas of what would cause her unhappiness." She bit on the inside of her lip. After all, Ellen *was* Mark's grandmother and she had no business interfering, even if she was only looking out for Ellen's welfare.

"I guess it's none of my business." She poked the vegetables on her plate with her fork. It was not like her to back out of an argument, but he was Ellen's grandson and maybe she'd overstepped her mark. Still, she resented his attitude.

"I appreciate your concern," Mark said, his voice still on this side of freezing. "But as you say, she's my relative, so I should know."

Nikki ate her meal conscious of a chilling silence in the room. The shifts between electrifying awareness of each other and cautious breeziness of the last hour or so had vanished, never to return, or so it seemed to her. Fifteen minutes later, she got up. "Excuse me. I have to wash up."

"And I have to get back to work," Mark said, pushing his chair back and getting up. He could get around faster than he had in the past several weeks.

Realization struck Nikki like a steam engine charging at her full tilt. He didn't really need her around–he could just as easily find a temp to do the work she did, somebody who wouldn't irritate him with lofty ideas of what should and shouldn't be done. She was free to leave, and Nikki knew she needed to get away from him for her own good, to remain heart whole.

She tried not to let her thoughts show, placing the dishes briskly in the sink before putting the food away in the refrigerator. If Mark ever guessed how he made her feel, she didn't know what she'd do. Could a person die from embarrassment?

Mark entered the kitchen and almost tripped as he skipped out of her way, obviously eager to leave the company of an opinionated housekeeper like herself.

"Would you like some coffee?" Nikki asked.

"Just leave a pot of it on the countertop before you leave. I'll rinse it out when I'm finished." Mark turned back for a fraction of a second and then strode out the door.

Nikki did her chores like a marathon contestant. She had a lot to think about, and she wanted to get to her apartment and have a cup of Earl Grey tea while she mulled over her future as Mark's employee and the business that was looming just around the corner, not to mention the inconvenient feelings that pounded in her heart and mind. She knew what they were and didn't want to give them a name; if she didn't acknowledge her feelings they would go away, she reasoned.

The final dish washed, Nikki wiped down the counter, set the coffee brewing in the coffeemaker, and muted the lights, leaving just one on.

"Goodnight," she called in the direction of the den and walked into the foyer to enter her own apartment. Once inside, she kicked off her shoes, heaving a sigh of relief.

Mark thumped his way through his e-mail messages. Some were from clients, one from Ellen, another from his father asking about the Renaissance project. Kyle wrote telling him the wedding was postponed and that Mark might still be able to be best man. So many messages, and he wasn't in a mood to concentrate. The one from Kyle made him squirm–he wanted no part of somebody's wedding at the moment. He wasn't being a grouch, he reasoned, but just didn't feel this was the right time. Mark decided not to send a reply right away.

He got up to fetch a cup of coffee and went into the kitchen. It smelled fresh and clean. Nikki did a damn good job of keeping house. An image of him coming home every evening and finding her dressed in a short skirt and a clingy blouse, making her look like a tasty dish, crept into his mind.

127

He wanted Nikki to be more aware of him, not just as a boss but as a person. She wasn't totally oblivious to him; their kiss proved that, but she was a prickly pear. Her discourse on moving Ellen out of her home had surprised him. What was that all about? Women!

Mark poured himself a cup of fresh-smelling coffee and headed back to the den. He was doing all right moving around, and he felt good about that. Didn't have to lean on his luscious housekeeper any longer, thank goodness. What *that* did to a man wasn't fit to print!

Once back at his perch on the stool, he cupped his face in his hand and stared at the messages that seemed like so much gibberish. All Mark could think of or see was the passion in Nikki's eyes when she spoke her mind about his grandmother and her home.

CHAPTER EIGHT

"This is just what we want," Mark said, glancing over the news release Dave was about to send to the *Tribune*. "It describes what the Renaissance project is about and, with a set of follow-up photos, it'll get all the publicity it deserves. And we're ready for a new name–"Renaissance Court." He grinned at Dave. "Great team work."

"It's been fun," Dave said. "Granted, we had some sleepless nights wondering if it was going to get off the ground as planned, what with tricky zoning regulations."

"Hope my grandmother likes it when I show it to her as a surprise." Mark felt like a child conjuring up a secret delight for his grandmother. Of course she'll like it–what's not to like about a spanking new condo with all the latest facilities? He felt as if everything he'd done all these years in his work converged into this one great present for Ellen, for all her loving care of him.

"Don't see why not." Dave put the sheet away carefully in his shiny folder. "It's the latest in streamlined design, combining practicality with style."

Mark threw back his head and guffawed. "You sound like the top-notch promoter that you are. But yes, I have to agree with you there."

"Good. Lunch?"

"No, thanks. I'm having Lois bring me a sandwich," Mark

said. "Feels great to be back at my own desk. I'd rather just stay here and work."

The weeks at home with his leg propped up had been hard. He had managed to get some work done, but there was nothing like getting into the nitty-gritty of things at the office–negotiating prices with vendors and talking to clients with facts and figures only a keystroke away. Of course, he did some of it at home, but there were too many distractions–all of them looking like Nikki.

When Dave left, Mark sat back in his swivel chair and gazed out at the golden tinge of autumn shining through the glass walls. He had missed the office and his work–there was a sort of excited anticipation in everyday meetings and targeted output of construction detail. Maybe that's why he'd been so cranky during the time he spent at home. No, that was not quite true–it had something to do with Nikki as well, and he didn't want to admit it to himself.

He propped his leg up on the desk and took a swig of freshly brewed coffee. He'd gotten into the habit of propping his leg up even when he didn't need to–it helped him think. He grinned to himself. Yeah, right. Think of Nikki.

Since the disastrous dinner two weeks ago when she'd scolded him about moving Ellen out of her home, they hadn't had dinner together. She'd finish her work and charge out of the apartment as if a bull was after her. Whatever drove her, she wouldn't tell him. She was busier than a squirrel gathering nuts for the approaching winter.

Yesterday, when she came into the den to tell him that dinner was ready, she'd looked like one of those playboy centerfolds photographed in subdued lighting. Oh, what was he thinking? He couldn't even remember what she was wearing, for God's sake. Lights had a way of playing tricks on a man. Then there were those feelings he'd been having each time she'd brought him a tray with sandwiches and coffee whenever he preferred not to have dinner while he sat looking at new design software. Almost like being...he hated using the "M" word, but he had to admit there was a comfortable feeling to whatever came over him. Sort of like knowing somebody was there, and that that person took care of him. No, strike that. Like having someone that meant something to him moving about in the kitchen. Did that sound like a wife? God forbid! But there it was–he couldn't lie to himself whatever he kept well-hidden from Nikki.

Mark brought his legs down and stood up. He let out a breath he didn't know he was holding–he always did that when thinking of Nikki.

It took him a few moments to realize the phone was ringing off the hook, causing him to break off from his thoughts and turn around. Mark picked up the phone. "Hello? Well, what a surprise, Marnie." His stepmother was back from goodness-knows-where, and had decided to give him a call.

"To what do I owe this honor?" he said.

"Mark, you've been neglecting your old stepmom." She sounded coy.

"You're not old, and you know it." And how she knew it; she'd come on to him on more than one occasion. That was all he needed–a stepmother with a crush on him.

"Do you really think so?" The coyness cloyed on him now, it was the difference between light-hearted banter and angling for undeserved compliments.

"Is there anything I can help you with?" A professional touch in his dealings with Marnie was the only way out of a tight spot such as this.

"I hear you have a new cook."

"She isn't new. She's been with me since Mrs. Babbitt left last spring," Mark said, wondering what she was getting at.

"I'm hosting a party, a barbecue...the last one before we start fencing up the bushes and preparing the lawn for winter. I thought some Japanese lanterns, musicians and some..." She was off into a description of what she had in mind. "...and wondered if I could borrow your cook—what's her name?"

"Nikki. She's paying her way through cooking school, so she's not your average housekeeper." Mark frowned a little at Marnie's odd request. Surely, she had plenty of help. What was she up to? "What about your regular cook?"

"Anthony's taking time off—something about seeing his relatives in Louisiana. He's never asked for time off before, so I had to let him go."

Mark could see Marnie sulking at the usual run of inconveniences that came with being the lady of the mansion. A broken fingernail would constitute a major calamity.

"You'll come, too?" she said. "Sorry about the late invitation, but I was away. Say you'll come, and bring the cook."

Mark gulped down a retort. It was just like Marnie to assume people would leave everything and run to do her bidding. But if she genuinely needed help with the barbecue, he'd better go to the assistance of a family member in need.

He shook his head in exasperation. "I'll see what I can do."

"You'll come, too?"

"Can't promise, but I'll try."

Not only did he need to ask Nikki to help out at Marnie's barbecue, but her service would be needed at the Grand Opening of the Renaissance Court building when he planned to have an Open House there. Would she agree? He couldn't tell.

For one thing, the way she kept out of his way told him she had something on her mind, but what? Maybe she just plain didn't like him. But the way she'd kissed him belied that. He looked away and let out an exasperated grunt.

When he reached home that evening, Mark found Nikki leaving his apartment.

"What, done already?"

"Yes," she replied. As usual, her hair was mussed and her face was flushed. Chores seemed to do that to her.

"I have an appointment to meet someone about renting space. Your dinner is ready. It's a vegetable casserole with garlic bread and braised pork."

"Sounds good. But I did want to talk to you about something. I was hoping you'd stay after the chores."

She clutched her purse under her arm like a quarterback on a football team and looked as if she was ready to dart out the door, except that he was in the way.

"Not now. As soon as I get back," she said, and vanished in the direction of the elevator.

Mark had to be content with that for now. He strode into his apartment and shut the door with a tired sigh.

Nikki rode the elevator down and got into her car, on her way to meet the manager of that terrific bit of space she'd seen not too far from Lincoln Park. She could just see her catering service taking shape there. A cooking range, microwave and convection ovens, and even a few tables and chairs for people who wanted something quick and were willing to wait while it was being prepared would add a definite personality to her business. It was in a choice spot, hence her rush to get there before somebody else gobbled it up.

Getting on the expressway, she took the fifteen-minute drive to the ultra-modern office building where Connie Pratt worked in City Planning.

Half an hour later, Nikki left the office holding an envelope containing the lease agreement of her catering business. She'd move in with Jenn, and she'd be all ready to start her new venture.

Now, she thought, revving up her car, what could it be that Mark wanted to talk about? Menus? Unexpected company? She was up to all that if it meant getting more experience for her new career, her lifelong dream. She intended to tell Mark one day soon. Not that she was being ungrateful to Ellen for getting her this job, or to Mark for taking a chance on an amateur housekeeper, but things were starting to heat up too much where Mark was concerned, and it bothered her.

Her old nemesis of being wary of rich men still intruded into her thinking. Besides, she was too close to her dream of being independent of family wealth to throw away all the effort she'd put into it. Falling in love couldn't have come at a more inconvenient time than the present. She drove away staring blankly at the road ahead of her, lost in thought.

The neon lights in the lower-deck parking lot of the Tivoli Apartments cast a pool of pale light as Nikki parked and got out, just in time to see Mark walking to his sleek, silver Lexus.

"You're back," he said, stopping and turning toward her. "Now, maybe we can talk."

"Now? Aren't you going somewhere?" Nikki thrust her keys into her jacket pocket.

"I am. But it's a place I want you to see."

"Me?" Nikki was puzzled. What was he talking about?

"Yes. If you have some time now, why don't you get in the car and I'll take you there."

Nikki was intrigued. Mark seemed to harbor a suppressed excitement; this was obviously something he was pleased about.

"Okay. Count me in."

He held open the car door for her and she got in.

"Hold on to your hat. Here we go." Mark deftly steered the car out of the parking deck and onto the highway.

"Are you going to tell me where we're headed?" The suspense was more of the needling variety than baffling–it was like being blindfolded and taken somewhere.

"If I just told you, it wouldn't have the right effect."

"You wouldn't be kidnapping me, would you?" Nikki seriously considered the possibility. And why not? Things had taken a turn in her own outlook in a way she hadn't anticipated. She had fallen for the guy whose house she cleaned, just like in the movies. Maybe he wasn't an architect at all, but a criminal and was going to hold her for ransom. She made light of it in her own thinking, puzzled all the same.

"If I kidnapped you, it would be to a desert island," he said with a laugh. "No. Definitely not a kidnapping."

Something about the highway and the exit struck Nikki as being familiar.

"Where are we going? This is close to where I used to live," Nikki said. "My old apartment. The one you demolished."

"You won't let me forget that, will you?"

Mark swerved gently into a gracefully curving driveway and toward a tall building that now came into view. Its exterior lighting threw a pale pink color wash into bold relief, and the tall columns which stood guard at the front entrance resembled sentinels of some old-world Southern mansion. An enormous stucco wall alongside said "Renaissance Court."

He parked under the portico and turned to Nikki. "How do you like it?"

She let out a gasp of admiration. No doubt about it, the man was a wizard in the architecture business. The condo had elegance, grace, and just the right touch of flamboyance.

"Let's go in," Mark said, opening his door. He came around and held open the door for her.

"This is a nice piece of work." Nikki looked up at the imposing structure, "and I have to say it's much less of an eyesore than the old apartment building that used to be here."

"So am I forgiven for tearing it down?" Mark came around and stood by her, close enough that she could feel her elbow touching his side.

He was putting her on the spot, wanting a clean slate from her. She didn't know if she could do that yet. But then, she had done all right so far. She even had him to thank for where she was in her career, so maybe it was best to forget the last-minute scramble to assemble her life again.

"Forgiven," she said. "Besides, it was an old building. Who knows how long it would have stood the test of time?"

"I want you to see the inside." He steered her toward the entrance, holding her gently by the waist.

Mark unlocked the large, frosted-glass doors, stepped inside, and turned on all the lights with the flick of a single switch. They stood in an elegant lobby, complete with parquet floors and a winding staircase with white faux marble steps. The beige walls were decorated with modern paintings mounted in silver frames, causing the atmosphere in the lobby to glow and crinkle with ambiance. One wall had simulated daguerreotype murals of Chicago landmarks in the 1900s.

"A bit of national history," Mark said, noticing her staring at the art-laden walls.

"You've got good taste," Nikki said, when she finally caught her breath.

He moved closer. "I should hope so." His voice turned husky in a tone that gave her goosebumps. She tried not to notice the way the lighting reflected off his hair, causing it to appear even darker, as if that were possible. The bomber jacket he wore fit him to perfection. He was a good dresser, but that didn't mean a thing to him—whatever he wore looked natural on him, not as if he'd spent hours staring at himself in a mirror. She'd known a few men who were worse than women in their weakness for fancy clothes, so she should know. Mark looked dashing in a T-shirt and jeans, and just as comfortable in a suit.

Nikki jerked her head away. She wanted to get on with the tour or get home. For one thing, it was safer that way.

"Would you like to see the suites?"

"A quick tour would be nice."

Nikki wasn't sure what she really wanted. Was Mark trying to prove a point by bringing her here? Something to do with Ellen and the argument they had over her some weeks ago?

"You have to see the Aqua Fit pool and some of the other rooms set up for get-togethers." He pointed in the direction of a long glass-and-chrome door that led to the pool, which was well lit and had lounge chairs by it.

"The water temperature is an even seventy-five degrees all through the year," he said.

He led her back to the lobby and pointed to a large lounge, the Hospitality Room. "For parties, guest speakers, and meetings." It had cozy-looking furniture, card tables, a fireplace, racks full of magazines, and colorful oil paintings on the walls.

"And this," he said, going into a shop with glass counters and shelves, "is Candy Dandy."

Nikki looked puzzled.

"It's a sweet shop for fudges, chocolates, ice-cream, frozen yogurt."

"Who's going supply the sweets?"

He looked straight into her eyes, holding her with a steady gaze for a few seconds. "I was hoping you would."

"Me? What makes you think...?"

"After all, you're going to be opening a service. You could cater this as well. I'd be paying you, of course."

Mark led the way to his car and opened the door for Nikki. Waiting for her to settle in, he started the engine. "Now that I have your attention, there's something I need to ask you."

"Okay. I'm listening."

It had been a while since Nikki and he had talked. She'd caught a glimpse of him in the den, or talking on the phone to overseas clients, loudly if the connection was poor. But that was all.

"My stepmother, Marnie, is planning a big garden party. She wants you to help with the cooking. Her chef, Anthony, is visiting relatives in New Orleans. She's hired a temp to help with the barbecue, but wondered if you might be able to help, too. Would you mind?"

Nikki had half a mind to tell Mark about the lease for her catering business, but Marnie's assignment somehow choked it off. It was a means of earning extra money and, after all, what would he care about her bit of good news?

"Your stepmother? I don't think I've met her." Nikki glanced at him. She'd talked to his father over the phone, replying to inquiries when Mark was out. Housebound with his injured ankle, Mark answered his own phone calls, so she had not had further occasion to talk to Otto.

"Marnie's the ultimate social butterfly. She wants a last, big outdoor bash before boarding up for winter," Mark said with a sideways grin. "Have to admit the weather's been gorgeous, unseasonably warm for fall."

Nikki had to agree. "When is it set for?"

"This Saturday."

Today was Wednesday. "That's alright with me." She was in the catering business; she'd have to deliver at short notice. Whatever Marnie wanted her to do, it would be good training ground for her.

"Good. Then I'll let her know." He looked at her with an expression that puzzled her. "And Nikki," he said. "Thanks."

The aroma of barbecuing pork, chicken, and brats with the special glazing sauce that Nikki had concocted sifted through the mild evening air. The lush gardens at the Runyon estate were still green in the generously warm weather. The guests obviously were enjoying the Indian summer, while Nikki and the other barbecue chef prepared and served the food on elaborately decorated tables. Nikki straightened her apron, tied over black pants and a spotless white blouse, and glanced around.

"So you're the mysterious housekeeper who's been taking care of Mark," Marnie swayed up to the table where Nikki was patting a napkin into place.

Nikki looked up. She hadn't seen Marnie, and had assumed that she was busy chatting and drifting from one guest to the other. She wore a long, slinky pink skirt and tight black blouse. Her blond hair was caught up in a high pompadour, and she wore heavy make-up. She took a puff on her cigarette.

"I've been wondering where Mark's been hiding you."

"He hasn't been hiding me anywhere," Nikki replied with a laugh. "I've had my hands full, that's all."

"I hear you're going to open your own catering service."

"Yes."

Nikki was careful not to say any more than "It's something I've always wanted to do." She was not sure why, but she had a gut feeling she should be careful about what she said around Marnie. She had a strange, predatory look about her.

More than once, Marnie's gaze strayed toward Mark, who had Kenny by his side grinning up at him. A couple of women were chatting with him, and there was no mistaking the ardent looks they gave him.

Nikki abruptly looked away. She had no business watching him; she was on duty right at this minute. But try telling that to her heart, which was thumping like large raindrops in an empty drum. Forks slipped from her fingers onto the table and she grabbed them before anyone noticed. This wouldn't do; she'd better pull herself together.

"You must have a good head for business." Obviously, Marnie was going to stay around a while longer.

"I'll soon find out if I do or not." Nikki smoothed the end of the tablecloth that had lifted in the breeze.

"Well, I'm sure Mark will bail you out if you don't. You can always use his name for a reference." There seemed to be a world of meaning in her words, which sent a bolt of irritation through Nikki.

She looked steadily at Marnie. "If he does, it will be commensurate with my performance and skills. It's the least any employer can do."

"Don't get me wrong, honey." A half-smile lifted the corner of Marnie's over-painted mouth. "You seem capable and efficient. You'll get what you want."

An angry retort nearly sprang from her lips, but Nikki choked it back. Marnie's remark smacked of jealousy; maybe she was infatuated with Mark How odd, she must be quite a bit older than he was, and she was his stepmother to boot. Did Otto guess his wife had a crush on Mark? If so, what did he think, and did he care? Some men were blind to the antics of much younger wives–he probably fell into that category.

"What I want now is to make sure everything looks just right." Nikki moved one of the chairs so it wouldn't wobble.

"Oh, here you are, Mark," Marnie said, causing Nikki to lose her concentration and look up. Mark stood watching her intently. He had driven Nikki over and had not been too talkative–probably preoccupied with work.

"I was telling Nikki how capable she was," Marnie said in a silky tone. Nikki had the satisfaction of seeing a sharp look steal across Mark's face. It didn't look as if he was buying Marnie's butter-wouldn't-melt-in-her-mouth routine.

"Then I hope you're pleased with the results." Mark's face showed no expression. "Where's Dad?" He looked around.

"He's chatting with some old friends of mine," Marnie replied.

Something about the way Mark took in that bit of information told Nikki that he didn't care for any of Marnie's acquaintances. Was he as protective of his father as he was of Ellen?

"How about trying your hand at croquet?" he said to Kenny. Nikki was amused to see the boy's hair combed slick down, and that he was wearing tan trousers with a long-sleeved shirt.

"Yeah, sure," Kenny said, beaming.

"Go ahead," Mark said. "I'll join you in a minute."

Mark would make a good father someday. Just watching him with Kenny told her that. He had such a strong sense of family that she asked herself why he wasn't married. Watching him with Marnie, she wondered if his stepmother had something to do with that.

"Is Ellen coming?" Nikki said, avoiding his gaze.

"She might stop by later. She had a christening to go to before this."

Nikki smiled, thinking of the way Ellen spread herself around, energetic as always. But she probably wouldn't miss an opportunity to see her beloved Mark.

"It's been a while since I saw her." Nikki remembered their last meeting when Ellen asked if she was overworking herself. She glowed with warmth at the memory of it.

"That makes more than one person who's looking forward to seeing her," Mark said, looking in the direction of the croquet players before striding off to join Kenny.

"So Ellen got you the job with Mark, did she?" Marnie asked, refusing to go away.

"Ellen and I were in the same cooking classes. She knew I needed work."

"Wasn't that convenient! I hope you don't think Mark is easy prey. Other women have tried."

Including you? Nikki wanted to say. She worked alongside the tables, Marnie following her as she resolutely moved away. The woman was persistent. Nikki had to give her that. But why? Maybe she was a threat to Marnie in some way.

"Don't worry. I have a much fuller agenda than that," Nikki said, coolly. "Now, if you'll excuse me, I have to announce dinner."

"Nice chatting with you, honey," she heard Marnie say.

Nikki tried to ignore her prattle. She should have shaken Marnie off sooner, but she didn't want to appear rude. After all, she'd hired her for tonight's shindig, although it was a good guess that Marnie was curious to see Nikki and observe Mark interact with her.

A wry smile lifted her mouth as she thought about Marnie for a moment, and then shrugged to herself. Time to lead the guests to their tables.

"Ladies and Gentlemen," she said, "if you will take your places, dinner will be served shortly."

Amidst the bustle of people taking their seats, Mark walked up to Nikki with a heavyset, distinguished-looking man barreling alongside.

"Nikki, I'd like you to meet my father," Mark said.

"So you're the young lady who's been running Mark's apartment so efficiently," he boomed. Nikki couldn't recall his voice sounding like a foghorn to this extent, but telephones were deceptive.

"Nikki Slater. I'm pleased to meet you."

She liked him and immediately felt sorry for him, being married to Marnie, who probably ran the marriage and her own life the way she liked. What must it be like for a powerful man to be dominated by a much younger woman?

"Otto Runyon," he said, and pumped her hand. "Didn't expect to see someone so young and attractive." He peered at her for a moment. "Haven't I seen you somewhere?"

"I don't think so," Nikki replied, caught off guard by his question. He couldn't have been at one of the soirees that she and her mother had attended, could he? Nah. It didn't matter, anyway. People often mistook people for others. "I have an ordinary sort of face. The kind that people think they've seen somewhere else."

"Well, nice to meet you, young lady. I have to see to my guests." He looked around. "Now where has Marnie made off to? Here one minute, gone the next." He strode off, leaving

Mark grimacing at Nikki.

"Was Marnie giving you the third degree?" Mark shot her an apologetic look.

"She all but asked me if I had designs on you." Nikki laughed, but she was feeling far from jocular. It was one thing for women to feel that Mark was their personal property, but it was another for Marnie to suggest that Nikki had ulterior motives for being in Mark's employ. Besides, her feet hurt, her head ached from the smoke of the barbecue, and all she wanted was a hot shower and to soak her feet in Epsom salts.

"I'm sorry about that," Mark said. "She can't quite forget her life as a showgirl in Las Vegas, so she's still in a state of wonder at having married my father, who can't see any wrong in her." Nikki nodded as if in agreement, yet couldn't help wondering what that had to do with Marnie's possessive attitude toward Mark.

As people took their seats, Nikki moved away to the serving area. She didn't want to appear conspicuous talking to Mark, since she was only the hired help. How odd, since she was used to garden parties where prominent names dropped like leaves in the fall. This didn't seem any different, except that she was one of the servers. When her parents had their garden parties catered, she used to feel sorry for the long hours the domestic help put in. She didn't need to empathize any longer; now she knew from experience. She flexed her toes insider her tight shoes. She also knew she'd never play the part of the boss lady cracking the whip.

From her station, Nikki saw Mark take his place between two sleek women, and her heart thudded in a pang of jealousy. So much for her keenly honed professionalism.

Two hours later, Mark came by to give her a ride back to her apartment. Nikki had just finished helping to pick up and stack the empty dishes and silverware in the kitchen. She took off her apron and shook it out. Flushed from her duties, she was happy to be going home.

She clutched an envelope that Marnie had thrust into her hand, and when she looked inside, Nikki found a check for two hundred dollars written in a large, flowery handwriting. She'd earned her salary today, no doubt about that.

"You must be bushed," Mark said, as he steered the car out of the Runyon estate and on to the highway.

"Yes, it's been a long day."

Mark looked at her. "Thanks for the help."

She nodded, too tired to say anything, only wanting to get home.

Nikki checked the lasagna in the oven and wiped her hands on her apron, sniffing the tangy aroma with satisfaction. The garlic toast was ready and waiting, covered in a red-and-white checked cloth napkin and cradled in a designer breadbasket. Now for the salad. She took out lettuce, tomatoes, and a cucumber from the fridge.

For a moment, she didn't hear the doorbell ring. Then it rang again, this time with a shrill persistence. Nikki glanced at her wristwatch—four-thirty. Too early for Mark to be home from work; besides, he wouldn't ring the doorbell since he had the key. A salesperson? Well, she could send him away in short order.

Nikki hurried through the hallway and pulled open the door. Her hand still resting on the doorknob, she expected to see a briefcase-toting salesperson, but a very different person stood there, patting her just-styled hair.

"Mother," Nikki said, surprise knocking the wind out of her. "Imagine seeing you. What are you doing here?"

"I would like to talk to you, Nicole." Her mouth set in a grim line. "I always seem to miss you when I call your apartment, all I get is the answering machine. You don't know how off-putting that is. May I come in?"

Nikki took a deep breath. She had to finish cooking, Kenny was going to be dropped off by his mother, and Nikki had promised him dinner. There had been no time for that glorious outdoor picnic in the ripening fall weather because she had been too busy running around making arrangements for the equipment she needed to open her catering service.

"Matter of fact, I'm in the middle of making supper. Mark has invited a friend over. But come on in." She led the way to the kitchen.

Nikki turned around. Her mother came up behind her, scrutinizing the apartment and seemingly taking note of its contents. She looked impressed.

"If he's anything like I've heard, he must be on top of the eligible bachelor list. And look at you," she said, shaking her head. "You're reduced to cooking for him. How could you do this to the Slater name?"

"Mother," Nikki said, firmly, "I'm not reduced to anything. I work here to support myself, and my catering service will open in a few weeks." She resumed her chores in the kitchen while her mother stood near the table, looking at everything with a critical eye.

"You're smart enough to go into banking yourself, if you chose to do so," her mother said.

"That's not what I want. I'm happy with what I'm doing." Nikki tried to concentrate on the lasagna sizzling in the oven. She was so near to opening her catering business, she didn't need her mother discouraging her now, well-meant as she was. Why couldn't life be simple, at least until she achieved her goal, which was almost within reach?

"You're selling yourself short. You could be the lady of this magnificent apartment, married to Mark Runyon," her mother said with a tinge of hope in her voice, something Nikki recognized from childhood. Mother could sound friendly and concerned when she wanted.

"How do you think I should go about it?" Nikki couldn't resist saying it.

"Play your cards right, and Mark Runyon will marry you."

"Marriage?" Mark's deep voice broke the momentary silence in the room. "Were you ladies talking about me? I didn't know you were in the market for a husband, Nikki. I could have warned you to look elsewhere."

CHAPTER NINE

Nikki spun around as if she had been zapped by lightning. Mark stood leaning against the doorframe. How long had he been standing there? How much had he heard?

"Mark!" She looked up, flushed with humiliation and embarrassment. "I didn't hear you come in." She held out her hand, palms upward. "I want you to meet my mother. She just dropped by." She managed to conceal the fact that she was out of breath from being caught off-guard.

Charm took over completely as if on cue, and Nikki's mother extended a ring-swathed hand. "So *you're* the Mark Runyon I've heard so much about."

"And I hope most of it was good," Mark said with a gallant smile.

But Nikki saw the hard, telltale set of his features; it belied the effort of his amiability. Goodness knows what he must have inferred from overhearing the conversation.

"Of course," her mother said, her voice dripping with sweetness. "Can you doubt that?"

She glanced at her watch with an air of someone who had numerous social obligations. "I must be off. Nikki, don't be a stranger to your mother."

The honeyed tone of a few moments ago was conspicuously absent when her mother talked to her. She turned to Mark. "So nice to have finally met you. Goodbye," she said, sounding genuinely pleased.

"I'll see you to the door," Mark said, following Nikki's mother into the hallway. Always the perfect host, Nikki thought. Now what? Would he be affected by what he'd overheard? It would depend entirely on the spin he put on it.

Nikki decided to make the salad; it would help to keep her hands busy while she tried to sort out the situation in her mind. Having been interrupted in her chores by her mother's visit, the vegetables sat on the counter like a colorful advertisement for healthy eating.

She tucked her hair behind her ear and then let out a sigh. It was going to be a long evening if Kenny was coming over and she had to sit through dinner pretending things were okay. On the one hand, she'd have loved to see the cheerful kid, so blissfully happy as long as he was around Mark; on the other hand, today was not the day for entertaining company. She'd sooner serve dinner and leave.

"What was all that about?" Mark returned to the kitchen. If the tautness of his features was any indication, he was clearly not pleased by what he'd overheard.

"My mother has a tendency to marry me off to any man I even talk to. She was reminding me that I should get married and settle down."

"That wasn't what I was referring to."

"What, then?"

Nikki grabbed tomatoes and cucumbers from the colander, glad to be able to have the vegetables to chop and slice. Standing still while being questioned would have been too much, especially under Mark's cold stare. His eyes, usually a warm, melting hue, were glacial now.

"That you're from money. From the wealthy Slater banking family," he said. "I thought you were a poor relation, trying to make ends meet."

Nikki looked up at him. "Would you have preferred that?" She needed to find out exactly what his objection was.

"At least that would have been an honest admission, instead of pretending you were paying your way through cooking school." Mark's gaze never wavered from her face. There was something statue-like in the way he stood there, and it intensified her sense of foreboding.

Awkwardness seemed to pull the air tight around them, and Nikki was quick to feel the thrust of it. She had to at least convince him that her motives had been completely honest, that she was no gold-digging adventuress.

"Look, I didn't want to accept financial help from my parents. That's not so difficult to understand, is it?"

"Choosing to make it on your own is a great goal, but hard to pull off." Mark moved to the sink and helped himself to a glass of cold water, which he gulped down in one long swig. "What I don't understand is why you couldn't tell me the truth."

He must have had a long, intense day, Nikki thought. His tie was loosened and his sleeves were rolled up. That seemed to be his trademark when he was very busy at the office. Funny that she should notice these little things about him—it was almost as if she could see in her mind's eye what kind of a day he'd had.

"I didn't lie to you."

"A lie of omission. Same thing."

"No matter how it sounded, I'm not setting my cap for you. That's not what this job was about. My mother has one goal, to see me married, but it's not my goal."

"You don't share her view?" Mark asked, his expression icy. She'd be lucky if he entertained one thought in her favor right at this moment.

"Of what?"

"Of thinking of me as a 'good catch.'"

Nikki flushed with annoyance and embarrassment. "Of course not! What do you take me for? Credit me with some pride and self-respect."

"You'll have to excuse me if I fall short of that much insight," Mark said. "I've just had something of a shock, remember."

"Meaning?" Nikki said, her breath coming in short spurts.

"Well, it's not every day an employer wakes up and finds his housekeeper has lied about her entire life. It's the stuff of fairy tales, as they say." He gave a dry laugh. "However, I don't need a housekeeper who lies to me, even a rich one."

"So I didn't tell you everything about my life. It doesn't mean I'm a liar. All I wanted to do was to make my own living, to get ahead by myself, not with the help of my family."

"Correction. You got your job because of my grandmother. And now when you see how hard it is, coming from your rich lifestyle, you think..."

Nikki didn't let him finish. "You think I'm trying to hook you to make it easy for myself?"

"Can you blame me?" Mark placed the glass on the table with a thud. "I know how women operate. I watched Marnie trap my father into marriage."

Nikki had just placed the vegetable casserole on the kitchen table when she stopped short, and her jaw dropped at Mark's words. So that was it! He put her in the same league as Marnie, who used goodness knows what means to get Otto to marry her.

Despite Nikki's outrage at Mark equating the two of them, she couldn't help seeing the comical side of the incongruity of this comparison. She couldn't be less like Marnie than if she'd turned into a rabbit by some magician's wand.

"Marnie?" Nikki said. "Are you saying I'm like *Marnie*? I don't know what happened between her and your dad, but I'm not up to anything you should be concerned about." She took a deep breath. She thought she knew Mark a little by now, knew him enough to trust that he wasn't like a lot of men, running scared at the sight of a woman, paranoid with fear at being "caught."

The metallic trill of the doorbell brought their face-off to a halt.

"That'll be Kenny. His mother is dropping him off." Mark strode off into the hallway to open the door.

This was the dinner she'd promised to prepare for Kenny, and she wanted to run to her apartment and remain there. She felt too heartsick to stay and be polite to Mark and Kenny, but Kenny would think it odd if she weren't there. How did everything come crashing down about her ears in so short a time?

A few minutes later, Nikki heard Kenny come running in like a frisky, overgrown colt.

"Hey," he said as soon as he saw Nikki. "What smells so good?"

"Lasagna." Nikki smiled. "Do you like lasagna?" What a foolish question, she thought. All kids liked lasagna.

"Yep. Enough to marry it." He grinned.

Mark had walked in quietly and stood near the door, arms crossed. "Are we ready to eat?"

"Yes," Nikki said. Too late to leave, she thought, especially now that Kenny was already here. "I've set the table."

Kenny was first to find a seat. Mark took his without comment and opened up his napkin. This was going to be one of those think-while-you-eat dinner sessions, because she wasn't in any mood to pretend to be the charming chef today and swirl the conversation around. Tomorrow would be different; tomorrow she would give notice to Mark in as diplomatic a manner as she could. She couldn't stand being here one more day, in Mark's presence, and have him question her motives for seeking this job. Thankfully, Kenny was full of the Chicago Bulls' latest victory, and Mark appeared just as engrossed in the highlights of each quarter of play. But Nikki had lost her appetite and the lasagna, delicious though it tasted, was left untouched on her plate. She hardly noticed the succulence of the cheese topping and the pasta.

Kenny seemed not to notice that the intricacies of the Bulls game couldn't be less interesting to her at the moment. "So, Nikki, when are you coming to watch a game with us?" Kenny suddenly turned bright, eager eyes on her, favoring her with a wide grin.

"I don't know," Nikki said, smiling. "I'm too busy."

"Nikki has a tight schedule." Gentleness characterized Mark's tone. "We mustn't force things on her."

He thinks the world of Kenny, Nikki thought, awash with misery. It was only her he was suspicious of, and he'd never get over feeling that way as long as she was in sight, day after day. Time to make your exit, Nikki, in more ways than one.

After dinner, Mark and Kenny disappeared into the den to watch videotapes of NBA playoffs while Nikki cleaned up. It being Friday, Kenny's mother had allowed him to stay out a little longer.

Rinsing the dishes, Nikki formulated a plan. She'd stay with Jenn until she found an apartment. After all, her business location was all set and her loan to buy the equipment had been approved. She was on her way. A few more weeks, and she'd have her diploma from the Institute. She'd explain to Ellen that it was important for her to move on, leaving the more personal details about what she felt for Mark carefully out of the scenario.

Nikki hurried to wash up; the sooner she completed her chores, the sooner she could beg off for the rest of the evening. Kenny would understand that she had her own work to do.

She smiled at the thought that intruded. Young Kenny was growing up to be a typical male, with all the usual hobbies. He was a good kid, though, and maybe he had Mark, his consistent role model, to thank for that.

Nikki felt every nerve stiffen as Mark sneaked into her thoughts. She had no business thinking of him now—much better if she forgot the feelings that were threatening to erupt. But now, things were bursting like a bubble floating in limbo. She couldn't base her feelings on a lack of trust, or an entirely different way of thinking between two people. She was so confused, she just wanted out. Thankfully, the end of this hopeless mission was in sight.

In half an hour, the dishes were rinsed and loaded in the dishwasher, and the table wiped clean. From the sounds she heard, she gathered that the guys were still in the den. She wiped her hands and headed that way. Mark looked up as she entered.

"I'm all done in the kitchen," Nikki said. "If there's nothing else, I'll be leaving."

"Okay." His voice hadn't lost its jagged quality, so he was still cold-shouldering her. Fine.

"Wait," Kenny said, looking up from the electronic gizmo he was playing with—one of those handheld games, Nikki guessed. "I got something for you." He handed her a small, white box.

"For me?" Nikki was surprised and touched by Kenny's sweetness.

He nodded. "Mark helped me pick it out."

Nikki flushed and glanced quickly at Mark, who looked amused. She opened the box and took out a delicate silver bracelet. "How sweet," she said, giving Kenny a hug. "Thanks. I'll always treasure it."

"Aw, that's great." Kenny grinned and wriggled out of her arms.

Where did he get the money from? Nikki wondered. As if reading her mind, Mark said tersely, "He bought it out of what he earned cleaning yards in his neighborhood."

Why did Mark feel he had to explain? To make certain that Nikki understood that he hadn't paid for it?

"I love it," Nikki said, taking the shiny bracelet out of the box and clasping it on her wrist. "But you shouldn't have wasted your money."

"That's okay. I'm sure glad you like it." He threw Mark a pleased look. "We did good, didn't we, Mark?"

"Sure did," Mark said with a poker face. He must have been roped into the job of helping Kenny choose a bracelet and was likely not pleased at having to do it. The immovability of his expression was witness to that. It must now seem a travesty to him–having had to select a bracelet for somebody rich, and who had everything she wanted anyway. That was probably what he was thinking.

Nikki gave a mental shrug as she tucked the small box into her pocket. Not much she could do about Mark's preconceived notions, now that he knew her background.

"Well, I'd better be off." Nikki took them both in with a glance. "Goodnight. Breakfast tomorrow, Mark?"

"Yes." His voice sounded as desolate as freezing rain.

Nikki walked out, her chin tilted up. She didn't want Mark to have even a glimpse into her thoughts. Her throat constricted as she left the foyer and opened the door to her apartment and leaned against it when she got inside. This was it–the end of one phase of her life and on to the next one. Anticipation lent her wings, and she soared with new hope at the thought of being her own master at last, but a niche in her heart throbbed achingly, and it spelled Mark.

Nikki opened the closet and took out her suitcases. She pulled clothes off their hangers and started folding them–her few belongings could go into the suitcases and the cardboard boxes she had brought them in. She'd known she'd be leaving some time but, as of today, the process had speeded up. She needed to give notice and leave as soon as she could. Maybe she'd stay a few more days until Mark found a temp; she'd tell him that. But her new job needed her. More than that, she had fooled herself into thinking that she had remained in this job solely for the money. Well, that had helped, but it was more than that. It was Mark. She needed to be around him, and it wasn't the right thing to do.

Nikki looked about the bedroom and felt a tug in her chest. She'd been happy staying here, attending cooking school and working for a decent salary. But her heartstrings were being pulled in different directions.

She picked up her hairbrush and absentmindedly ran it through her hair. She'd move in with Jenn, who'd only be too delighted to have her stay over until Nikki found an apartment. Jenn had always appreciated Nikki's company.

For the past few days, Nikki had been busy taking out ads in the *Tribune* and posting flyers in appropriate locations. She felt butterflies kicking something awful in her stomach, but the culprits were excitement and the exhilaration of getting her catering service under way. She even knew what she was going to call it—*Bon Vivant*, French for "the good life." She'd had too many instructors from French cooking schools not to be influenced by them just a little.

Nikki had talked to a couple of fellow students, Lori and Marge, about her venture, and they had expressed an interest in working for her before opening something of their own. The three of them had worked together in cooking demos before and had established a good rapport among themselves.

By the time she had had a long, leisurely shower, humming to herself, Nikki felt a little less discouraged about her run-in with Mark. She even bristled with slight annoyance now. Actually, it shouldn't have mattered to him that she had kept her background secret—she was only protecting her image as an honest-to-goodness working girl. Too bad if he didn't see it that way! Nikki bundled her wet hair in a towel and knelt at the dressing table to clear out the drawers.

Nikki awoke with a jolt and peered bleary-eyed at the clock. Six a.m. The slanting early morning sunshine tried to filter in through the drapes. She sat up and pushed away the hair from her eyes. After preparing and serving breakfast, she would tell Mark she had to turn in her resignation, that her catering service was ready to open.

Half an hour later, Nikki took a deep breath and headed toward Mark's apartment with a grim smile tugging at her lips. The foyer was a link between their separate worlds. She was comfortable in both, really, but whatever she did was to be her own decision and hers alone.

Opening the apartment door, she entered. Mark was probably getting ready to go to work. Meantime, the kitchen beckoned and there was breakfast to be prepared. Nikki got out the bacon and eggs and popped a few slices of toast in the toaster. Then she poured out a small glass of orange juice, put on the coffee, and heard the reassuring bubbling sound a few minutes later. The dining room table laid, she waited for Mark to come out, grab his toast, and gulp down his coffee the way he invariably did. He liked to have breakfast at the large dining table so he could go over reports before meetings first thing in the morning.

Mark strode in clutching his collar, a navy-and cream-colored tie obviously having gotten a stranglehold on him. His shiny hair sprang back from his head like a thick coif.

"Darn this thing. The Development Board at Northwestern wants me to sit in on a project proposal for their new Center for Performing Arts. They called this morning, so I have to hightail it over there, but this thing wants to choke me. Do you mind?" He stopped in front of her and threw up both hands in despair. In his hurry, he had tied a deft sailor's knot, or something that could well qualify as one.

Nikki suppressed a chuckle thinking of the intrepid architect, Mark Runyon, all thumbs when it came to tying a tie. Yet in the months she'd been here, she hadn't known him to be in this predicament. Maybe the Board meeting had caused the unflappable Mark to fast-forward his activities to a knotted finish this morning.

"I have debriefing meetings with my own teams first thing this morning." He shook his head. "Now I have to go off on a tangent to Evanston."

"Hold still, please," Nikki said, straightening his collar. A rare feeling struck her as she thought of her chore of the moment–tying Mark's tie like a wife, or like a Mom sending her kid off to school. Yet she was neither of those things.

A mixture of jumbled sensations shivered through her.

She couldn't tell exactly how it hit her–standing there so close to Mark, she got a whiff of his incredible aftershave, some spicy scent that seemed to knock her over and catch her off guard. Oh, she liked the fragrance, it was just that she couldn't concentrate on the tie. The collar and the top shirt button seemed to get in the way just when she got the knot right. She kept her eyes fixed on the light blue and white pinstriped shirt, the corded muscles all too apparent beneath it. Her fingers seemed to slip every now and then...and this was the morning she was going to give notice, all in good spirit. Would he wish her well in her new career?

Nikki felt his chin brush against the top of her head. Great, her fingers now refused to move at all, and here he was waiting for her to finish so he could swallow his breakfast and run. Discouragement suddenly pulled her down. Nothing was going as she had planned. All she could do was stand there wishing he didn't have to rush, that she didn't have the task of telling him she was leaving, that he wasn't so handsome, and that she wasn't standing so close.

"What's the matter?" Mark asked. "Don't tell me you're all thumbs, just like me."

She dared not look up, but she heard a hint of amusement in his tone that had her flushing guiltily. Standing only a breath away, how could he not sense the crazy thoughts that chased each other through her head?

"No, I've got it done," Nikki said calmly, mentally sighing with relief. The errant shorter tail of the tie had finally allowed itself to be coaxed through the loop without her having to touch any part of Mark's anatomy, close as he was, and feeling his clean, minty breath on her. "Just making sure it's okay. There," she said, giving the tie a final pat. "All set. Ready for breakfast?"

"Thanks for helping with my tie." He sat down at the table and munched on his toast, while holding up the coffee cup.

It had to be said now, Nikki thought. She had put it off long enough–better face the music of giving such short notice.

"Mark, I have something to tell you," she said, trying to sound matter-of-fact. He looked up at her, lines furrowing his forehead.

"*Hmm*?"

"I have to leave your service. My business is about to open soon, and I need time off to get ready for it." She waited for it to sink in.

"This is pretty sudden, isn't it? If I'd known, I'd have looked for a temp." He strained to turn around to look at her. "You're sure your decision has nothing to do with yesterday?" His tone was nonchalant and seemed too casual.

"No, of course not," Nikki said and wished she didn't sound so emphatic, as if she were contrite. "It's just that my catering service is about ready to open soon."

"I understand." He bit into his toast and shifted around the scrambled eggs with his fork. "I'll just have to get a temp. I've done that before. Maybe the employment agency..."

"I could stay a few days to help train the temp, if you like."

"Yes, that would help." He finished his coffee and then pushed away his plate. "Well, I hope you'll be happy in your new career, Nikki."

She glanced at him, wondering if he really meant it or if he was being snide. After all, she had sprung this on him out of the blue. His mouth set in a tight line, but his voice melted over her, smooth as ever. She could stand there staring at him forever, watching him lift his coffee cup as he glanced through the reports he carried with him to the dining table each morning. She'd better get herself in hand. They were two people who were now so wary of each other that it would take the wiliest diplomat to create an armistice between them. There was no room in her life now for heart-throbbing feelings for Mark.

Nikki pushed open the window and stuck her head out, sniffing the air. The fresh scent of crisp, cool air met her nostrils, and she inhaled deeply. Hopefully, fall would continue a while longer, holding the inevitable cold, gusty Chicago winds at bay. The window boxes outside the *Bon Vivant* still had a few blooming red- and peach-colored geraniums.

For a moment, she stood watching joggers and bikers on the path winding toward the lakefront. Another deep breath, this time with the satisfaction of seeing green open spaces nearby while, at the same time, watching restaurants and boutiques around Lincoln Park send people lolling in the direction of *Bon Vivant*.

Nikki turned away from the window. Successful though she was, a tiny bit of emptiness sabotaged her soaring optimism like a treacherous, hidden boulder lying in wait for an unsuspecting boatman. It had been several weeks since her catering service was up and running, and she hadn't heard from Mark, or seen him. The last few days at his place had been punctuated with chilly politeness, and he'd kept to his office for the most part. As she had promised, she stayed on a few more days to ease the temp into her duties, and then she'd left. She tried to maintain a show of civility when she left, and Mark had done the same, but it wasn't the Mark she'd come to know. In the end, she hadn't been able to ask him for a letter of reference to keep in her file. What was the point?

The last thing she remembered, getting into the elevator, was Mark's detached expression. That had dealt her a final blow more than if he'd been angry or outraged at her leaving so suddenly.

Nikki chased the thought out of her head. Why have regrets about leaving Mark's employ when it wasn't just that, and well she knew it. She couldn't allow herself to go all mopey; she had a job to do.

Nikki turned around. Customers came in to take a leisurely walk through the catering center, as Nikki preferred to think of it, and browse through the various cooking-related items that were available for sale. That had been her assistants' idea. This would draw in more business, they'd pointed out, and they had been right.

There was handmade pottery bought on consignment from local artisans, selected cookware and bakeware, and hard-to-find kitchen gadgets. The *Bon Vivant* also sold gourmet coffee and cookbooks.

The phone rang and Nikki hurried toward it, but Lori got it first. "Yes, we do wedding cakes," she was saying into the receiver. "We have brochures with designs and prices. You might want to stop by and look them over."

Nikki nodded at Lori in approval. Orders for business conferences, anniversaries, birthdays, and engagements had kept them busy almost as soon as they'd opened. The ads and flyers they had distributed were doing their job, as was word of mouth, and Ellen used her influence to publicize the merits of the *Bon Vivant*. Dear Ellen, Nikki thought. It had been a while since she had seen the older woman, but whenever Nikki could find a moment she'd call her. Nikki had no doubt Ellen had been disappointed that she had had to leave the job with Mark, but she had understood that Nikki was on her way to a new career. She had wished her young friend well, and offered her every support in the new venture.

Nikki glanced at Lori jotting something down on a notepad. An order?

When she was free, Lori said, "An order for a wedding cake. Somebody recommended us to them." She grimaced. "The only problem is, the wedding is next Saturday and we have the Reynolds business reception order to fill next week as well."

"Not a problem," Nikki replied. "The Reynolds party is early in the week. It'll take me a day to prepare and decorate the wedding cake, so we're okay." She was learning to properly allocate her time to the orders, thanks to her disciplined training at the Institute.

"The bride and her mother want to meet with you to decide on the cake," Lori said. "Here's the number to call."

Nikki took the note from Lori and made a mental note to call this afternoon when things slowed down in the office. She loved doing wedding cakes, felt confident preparing them. The only problem was they made her sentimental, and that was the last thing she wanted to feel right now.

The next morning, Nikki got out her order book and several sheets of cake designs and then waited for her clients to arrive. Half an hour later, two women walked in—the younger one looking so radiant that Nikki felt a surge of goodwill toward her. She smiled and guided them to a table. "We can sit here and look at some samples," she said. "Would you like some coffee?"

They accepted coffee, made themselves comfortable, and began to sift through a variety of cake designs. Nikki even let them taste a delicate frosting sample that she was in the middle of creating for another client.

The bride decided on a champagne wedding cake, with its pretty curves and lines. "This one," she said, obviously quite sure of what she wanted.

Nikki wrote up a work order and gave them a carbon copy. "For your records," she said. "Incidentally, how did you hear of our service?"

She liked to keep track of how her clients came to hear of the *Bon Vivant*. It was part of the marketing research she conducted just to keep tabs on how far she was able to reach prospective customers.

"Oh," said the bride. "My fiancé's friend recommended your catering service. His name is Mark Runyon."

CHAPTER TEN

"Mark Runyon?" Nikki asked. Her hands trembled as she caught the scatter of papers which had fallen from her grasp. Trying to pull herself together, she said, "You know him?"

"My fiancé, Kyle, does, and thinks the world of him," the woman said. "I met him only once. He said you worked for him before and that he recommended you highly."

She looked at Nikki, a curious expression taking over her still-girlish face. "You must be good in your work. He's not easy to please, from what I hear from Kyle."

Nikki took a deep breath before replying. She'd regained her composure enough to savor the complimentary remarks that her client attributed to Mark. She'd revel in it later, in private.

She allowed herself a smile. "That's good to hear." Understatement of the year, she thought, closing the order book and collecting her sheets of designs.

The champagne wedding cake, she told herself, was the important thing now. Not Mark, not the ache in her heart, not anything else.

She had to get out the design for the three-tiered masterpiece with its white frills and bows skirting the edging. She sighed as she leafed through her folder and found it. She studied it for a few moments–yes, this would be perfect. It would take her half a day to prepare the cake and another half a

167

day to decorate it, then she could take it to the reception hall in separate boxes and reassemble it there.

Nikki's clients made their down payment for the ingredients and then left.

She drew in a deep breath and put away her order book. Her assistants were busy in the kitchen preparing pate and finger sandwiches for a ladies' bridge party.

Nikki had her equipment all in place. There was even a small area prettily done up with potted flowers and white tables and chairs for people to sit and drink a cup of gourmet coffee while going over cake and pastry designs. Ellen had stopped in to offer her good wishes and congratulations when the *Bon Vivant* opened. "All the best," she'd said, giving Nikki a hug. She'd thoughtfully refrained from mentioning Mark, and Nikki hadn't said anything either.

Nikki smoothed back her hair and got to work on baklava, a dessert for a client's son's engagement party. No, she thought, she hadn't done badly for herself at all. She'd found an apartment half an hour from the *Bon Vivant*, although Jenn wanted her to stay on, saying she couldn't remember when she'd last enjoyed girl talk over endless cups of tea. Nikki had to agree with her friend on that, but after several weeks of camping out at Jenn's place, it was time to move on, much as she missed the late-night chatter. A career girl was what she'd wanted to be and she'd made it, on her very own. So what was missing from the equation that made things not seem quite right? She couldn't put a finger on it, more likely she didn't want to. It lurked somewhere in her subconscious and she knew it, but darned if she would give it a name, or a face.

Nikki stopped rolling the crust and stood back, resting her palm on the rolling pin. Powdery sprinkles of flour blotched her hands and she wiped them on her apron. The rolling and kneading by hand were therapeutic; she didn't have to think while she worked. All she had to do was watch the small diamond-cut rolls take shape under her hands. No wonder catering gave her such pleasure; she created culinary wonders which delighted others.

A voice crept into her mind and blew the words, "Mark recommended you to the bridal party." And would he have done that if he hadn't thought her a good cook? Actually he would have, the stern voice told her, if he had wanted to appear conciliatory to make up for his accusations. Whatever! She didn't want to parade all that through her mind now.

Nikki stepped back and surveyed her handiwork on the display table. It amazed even her, the way the three tiers of the cake had turned out. Each layer had the palest pink and aqua roses, the edging flowing in delicate swirls like the frothiest bridal veil. On the topmost layer stood a miniature bride and groom under a small bower decorated with tiny colored swirls in the shape of roses. Would somebody prepare a cake like this for her someday? Now, why was she thinking like that when she hadn't even found a groom? And where did that thought sneak in from?

The sight of the beautiful cake in front of her jerked her back to the present, and her usual efficient self took over. Enough admiration of her work of art, she thought, and placed the three layers in the refrigerator where she had cleared pace for this purpose. There the cake would remain until Saturday, two days from now.

Meantime, she wanted to go and check out the reception hall where the dinner would be held. She had to see where she should place the cake, and it wouldn't hurt to look at the seating arrangement to get the general layout of the hall beforehand.

"I'll be out for a while," Nikki called out to her assistants working furiously in the back room unloading cardboard boxes containing special-ordered saucepans and Dutch ovens. "Could one of you watch the front while I'm gone?"

"Sure," Marge called. "See you later."

Shouldering her purse, Nikki walked to the small parking lot out back, got into her car, and swung out onto the expressway. She placed the directions to the reception hall on the dashboard and glanced at them now and then as she headed toward the Marriott. She had no idea how big it was, but wanted the cake she had labored so lovingly over for so long to have a prominent place in the hall. She wanted the bride to be happy with it on her special day.

Nikki walked into the plush-carpeted hotel lobby, checked the directory on the wall for the reception hall, and followed directions. As she passed her reflection in the gilt-edged mirror, she gasped—she looked dreadful from a day of hard work, but she shrugged to herself...so what? Who could she possibly run into that would even know her?

The reception hall doors were thrown wide open and she stepped inside, only to find it was full of people dressed in formal attire, all seated at tables. At the table closest to the aisle and only a few feet from her sat Mark, staring at her with a look of amusement. But that wasn't all. Next to him sat a smoldering brunette beauty dressed in a frothy off-the-shoulder number, practically hanging onto his arm.

What had she walked into?

"Can I help you?" One of the hotel staff appeared at her elbow.

"I'm catering the wedding cake for the Landon reception on Saturday," Nikki said firmly. "I wanted to check out the hall to see where the cake would be best displayed."

"This is the Landon party," he said. "The rehearsal dinner."

"Oh." Well, how was she to know that? Maybe she could come by later when it was over.

"If you come into the manager's office, I could give you a copy of the floor plan of the hall. That way you could get an idea of the layout."

It was better than nothing. Nikki threw a sideways look at Mark. He was Kyle's friend, so naturally he'd be here. The woman sitting with him was probably his date.

Now that she had straightened it all out in her mind, she wanted to get out of there as fast as she could, especially since she felt the charge of Mark's gaze still on her. The high-pitched voice of his companion cut through the low hum. "Mark, call the waiter, will you?" she said. "I want a refill on my drink."

Nikki tried to ignore the sharp twinge of jealousy coursing through her, making her face flush. What did it matter? When she thought about it calmly, she realized this woman was his date for the reception dinner and he had to be attentive to her, but knowing that didn't ease her-churning feeling. It was there, all right. Well, he was welcome to his female companion of the evening, Nikki had a floor plan to pick up and then leave.

Mark leaned back in his chair to get a better look at Nikki and what she was doing. For a nanosecond, his heart had seemed to stop and then it pounded like a hammer on an anvil when he spotted her standing there in her trademark daily wear of shirt and jeans. He'd felt his mouth go dry. Only he knew how much he'd missed her–the efficient no-nonsense ways, the sudden smile that lit up her face, and the hint of a dimple near her mouth which he had to remind himself not to think about.

And when he happened to turn around to talk to the guy at the next table, there she stood.

The sight of her arrested his attention, and their eyes locked for what seemed an eternity. It took a superhuman effort on his part to drag his gaze away and continue chatting with the others at his table. His date, the maid of honor, seemed to want to claim his attention unnecessarily and it was driving him crazy. Now she wanted a refill on her wine, so he snagged a waiter hurrying by.

"Wine refill here, please," Mark said. There, he'd done his job. He fidgeted with his cocktail glass. If only he could slip out of here and go after Nikki. But she had moved into the hallway, deep in conversation with an attendant. Something to do with the cake, no doubt. Of course! That was it. She was probably catering the cake for the wedding. Thoroughgoing professional that Nikki was, she'd want to check out the venue for the reception.

Dinner over at last, Mark drove to his apartment and thought things over. Seeing Nikki again after parting ways so abruptly had rekindled all the old feelings he had for her. He'd kept these feelings under wraps to manage them better—it wouldn't do to show her anything but a casual, mild flirtation, which he'd stir up with any attractive woman he encountered on a given day.

He let himself in and threw the keys on the carved walnut side table in the hall, glad to be in his comfortable bachelor quarters again. A wedding rehearsal was all very well, but a man needed his privacy to take stock of his own life situation, and see where it was going. Strange thing though, business was better than ever. His social life, on the other hand—well, he was dating now and then, but had never been able to connect with any of the women he met. The more stunning they were, the less they seemed to appeal to him. Nikki...now there was the perfect woman. Although he had to admit that finding out she had lied had been a shock, not what she had lied about, just that she had lied. He probably didn't have the right to judge her too harshly. Who knew how people's lives went and what they were forced to do?

He drew impatient fingers through his hair. This ruminating was getting him nowhere. He strode to the bedroom, shrugged out of his jacket, and pulled out jeans and a T-shirt from the closet. He'd left the reception a little early because he wanted to call Gran. It was finally time to spring his surprise on her–that he wanted to move her out of the old, drafty house to a spanking new condo in the livelier part of Chicago. He couldn't wait to see her face when he told her the news.

Mark changed quickly, picked up his cell phone, and dialed his grandmother's number. He heard a click and then her energetic voice came over the line.

"Hello, Gran," he said with a smile. It had been a while since he'd seen her and he hated that, because when they spoke she could be riotously funny and God knows he needed that these days. All work and no play...

"So nice to hear from you, Mark," she said. "Are you taking care of yourself?"

"Yes." He'd have to get to the topic of his mission quickly before she made this a Mark's-welfare chit-chat. "I have a surprise for you."

"Surprise?"

"The condo is ready and it's my present to you." He waited a moment and then continued. "It's just the place you need. It's in town and you can leave that old house in which you've been staying." Mark held his breath, waiting to hear her

173

pleased surprise.

"The condo?" His grandmother sounded puzzled. "I have a perfectly good house, Mark. Why would I want to move?"

"That's an old house, Gran. I'm not even sure it's up to fire code standards."

"I had the old wiring removed and new wiring put in."

"I'm glad you did that. But wouldn't you like to stay in the city where you can be close to the action?"

"At my age I have all the action I can handle."

"Gran, the new setup will be good for you."

She sighed. "Well, I'll think about it." She sounded tired, and suddenly, guilt invaded his gut.

"You'll like this new place, I promise you," he said.

As they chatted about other things, Mark noticed that the buoyancy had gone out of his grandmother's voice, so he hung up soon after. He fidgeted with the cell phone, staring moodily and wondering if he'd been right in expecting his grandmother to move to a brand new place without consulting her first. If, maybe, Nikki could have been right about pushing Ellen in a direction she didn't want to go.

God, how did he get himself into such a fix, first with Nikki, and now his grandmother. What was wrong with him? He'd felt edgy ever since Nikki left. Oh, he had the temp come in and she did good work, but the trouble was that he expected to see Nikki walk out of one of the rooms pushing the vacuum cleaner.

He remembered the eye-catching curves filling her jeans to perfection and the way her blond curls fell over her lovely eyes, which seemed to look deep into his soul as if she knew very well what was hidden there. Yeah, fat chance, when he himself didn't know what was in his soul.

He let the cell phone slip out of his hand onto the bed.

Nikki and Ellen were both somehow tied to his psyche. His grinding suspicions had sent Nikki away, but Ellen was still there for him, thank goodness.

All of a sudden, a fresh idea struck him. This one *couldn't* go wrong. He'd make amends for suggesting to Ellen that she move out of her old house; she was all the real family he had, and he didn't want to hurt her, he only thought the move would be best for her. How could he have been so blind?

Picking up his cell phone, Mark strode into the den and looked up Dave Roth's home phone number. He should know it by now, but he was too frazzled to remember phone numbers at the moment. Dave's project coordinator duties extended until the units were all taken.

He dialed the number and waited.

"Dave?" Mark said, hearing his loud, cheery voice. "Change of plan about the condo for Ellen Carstens."

"Your grandmother?"

"It'll still be hers, but only when she comes into town and wants to stay the night. Otherwise, she'll be in her old home."

"What happened?"

"I didn't have the good sense to ask her opinion, is what happened," Mark said wryly. "I just assumed she'd be happy to move." He shook his head. "But the condo stays furnished."

That done, Mark heaved a sigh of satisfaction. He'd never be this heavy-handed again, he vowed to himself silently.

That's it, Nikki thought, I'm sending Lori to attend to the cake on Saturday. She was busy rolling out the dough for scones, which would have rich cream filling inside. It was an English recipe she'd gotten from Colleen, one of her classmates at the Institute. Colleen swore by crumpets and scones for "high tea." Nikki smiled to herself. If she ever had a family, she'd invite her friends and her children's friends to high tea–it seemed such a charming custom.

Nikki wiped her forehead with the back of her hand. Charming custom or not, what made her think of having her own family? The wedding rehearsal. She rolled the dough with renewed vigor. What an idiotic thing to be thinking about when she had a flourishing business as the culmination of her lifelong dreams.

A knock sounded on the large, glass window separating the cooking area from the display room in front. The glass shelves were filled with every kind of chocolate fudge, white chocolate, pastries, and sample cakes for every occasion.

"Ellen!" Nikki smiled, a surge of warmth coursing through her. It had been eons since she'd seen Ellen. How she'd missed the conversations they'd had since Nikki graduated from the Institute!

"I've been trying to contact you." Ellen walked into the room and looked around her, then she gave Nikki a hug. "You'll get flour all over you," Nikki said, laughing.

"Let me look at you," Ellen said. "Young lady, I've missed our chats. How are you?"

"Busy, as you can see."

"You've lost weight."

"No time to eat. I've had more orders than I can fill," Nikki said. "You know my assistants out front, don't you?"

"Yes. They're very nice. But you need to get out more, or you'll end up like a dahlia bulb hibernating in the cellar."

Nikki sighed. She did miss some of the fun things she used to do–going window shopping with a friend, munching an ice cream cone, watching the boats plying Lake Michigan, or just plain doing nothing. And that wasn't all that was bothering her.

"Have you seen Mark?"

Nikki looked at Ellen sharply. "No—why do you ask?"

"Because of the way you left when he found out who you really were."

"No. I just had to move on. It isn't such a big deal, really. Actually, I ran into him at a wedding rehearsal dinner, where I'm catering the cake for his best friend's wedding."

Nikki practically had to drag the words out of her mouth. She loved Ellen, but didn't want to pour out her feelings all over her like spilled milk.

"Aha, now we're getting somewhere." Ellen sounded triumphant. "Ellen will cure you of what ails you. Let me ask one of my friends to introduce you to some nice young men."

"No, really. Actually, Brian—remember him from class? He has been bugging me to go out with him."

"You don't sound too thrilled."

"Oh, he's a nice guy." It was true. A little intense maybe, just when Mark was too much on her mind. Brian's pursuit of Nikki egged her on in the opposite direction. She finally decided she might go out with him just once and pretend to be a kleptomaniac or something to scare him off. "Don't worry, I'll be okay."

"I'm sure Mark misses you."

"Oh, Ellen, stop. He's not the type to miss anyone. I'll be all right, really." Nikki was alarmed that Ellen was taking all this so seriously.

They'd had some talks when Nikki had first opened her business, about how Mark had taken the fact that Nikki was from money and how he thought she had been deceptive and how he'd reacted. But she didn't want a repeat of their discussions; she wasn't imagining the dullness she felt now.

Saturday morning, Nikki pulled at the cord to open the drapes in the bedroom of her apartment and stood staring at the bright, sunny, snowy scene outside. It was a mixture of tall, imposing maple trees, the tops of snow-covered houses, and just barely a glimpse of Lake Michigan in the distance. She took a deep breath, pulled her robe tightly around her, and pattered into the kitchen to make coffee.

Minutes later, armed with a steaming cup of coffee and the paper she'd retrieved from outside her front door, she settled on the sofa to relax. She sipped her coffee and let it dribble down her throat, savoring its rich flavor as she looked around the living room. Her new apartment was comfortable, functional, near work, and she had filled it with bric-a-brac she'd collected—wall hangings, paintings, lamp shades that had screamed to be bought from galleries and antique stores. And her business was picking up. So why did she still have that empty, dug-out feeling in her stomach? The prospect of seeing Mark again at the wedding reception—that was the culprit.

Seeing him there the other day, staring at her and looking more handsome than ever in a tux, had sent shivers through her. Was it the tux, or him? She couldn't tell. The brief second that their glances had interlocked seemed to snap and sparkle with a hidden fire. It didn't matter that there was a hall full of guests causing an immense din of background noise. Wearing her black and white uniform, she couldn't bear to tend the cake in his near vicinity while he sat there with his date, or whoever he was escorting, probably the maid of honor.

Nikki arrived at the *Bon Vivant* an hour later and set up her table to start taking orders for the day. Lori was packing an order for a customer. There were only the two of them there today—it was Marge's day off.

"Could you take the cake to the Landon reception today?

I have all these orders to fill." Nikki shot Lori a bright look and waved her hand toward a stack of orders stuck on a needle at the center counter. Hopefully, Lori wouldn't sense that Nikki didn't want to go or that she wanted to avoid seeing somebody there.

"I wouldn't mind going." Lori folded wax paper neatly into a box. "But I'd feel like I'm doing nothing while you're working hard here."

"No, no. Go." Nikki waved both hands at her. "It will be good publicity for the business for people to see somebody else besides me every time." That much was true.

Hers was a fledgling business with a staff of three, but it was thriving. The way it was going, maybe she could even hire a couple of more assistants.

"Well, that's true." Lori appeared convinced. "I'll go get the boxes to pack them in."

They went into the back room where the cake stood ready in a stiff plastic cover which Nikki had devised. Nikki had put on the finishing touches late last night and had left for her apartment, satisfied that she had done her best. She removed the cover now and Lori gasped.

"It's beautiful!"

Nikki took a step back, cocked her head to one side, and gazed at the three-tier wonder in front of her. She couldn't help feeling a tinge of pride as she gazed at the wisps of pink lace icing woven into scalloped curlicues.

Lori brought the white boxes and placed them on the long table. Wearing thin, clear plastic gloves, Nikki gently dismantled the tiers one by one and placed them into the boxes, ready to be taken to the reception hall.

At noon, the blue and gray van with the *Bon Vivant* sign blazoned across its sides stood waiting at the back entrance, while Nikki and Lori carefully carried the boxes out and placed them in the flat area in the back.

"There," Nikki said. "All ready to go." She returned to her workspace littered with open bags of flour and sugar, measuring cups, and small vials of vanilla essence. Pulling a plastic cap over her hair, she got to work.

Nikki kneaded, pounded, and turned the dough—she could have used her dough-maker for this, but she wanted to do it by hand. There was something about working by hand that slowed her pulse and calmed her down. Nobody would miss her at the reception and she needed to work out her frustrations. Lori would do a nice job of setting up the cake and helping to serve it after the bride and bridegroom cut it and pictures were taken. She had escaped running into Mark again. Wasn't that the most important thing for her at the moment? Sure it was.

Several hours later, the sweet aroma of baking filled the bright, airy kitchen, and Nikki started washing and putting away pots and pans. She scrubbed the table and wiped it clean, and scoured the sink. Where she got the energy to go at it all day, she didn't know, except she loved her work. Maybe that was it.

A tap on the long windowpane had her looking up, puzzled. She was closed and not expecting any customers at this hour. Nikki felt her mouth form an "O" of surprise—there stood Mark, waving at her and pointing at the door.

She pulled the door open. "Mark! What are you doing here?"

He walked in. "I've come straight from the reception. Dancing's about to begin, and I'd like you to come back with me."

"Are you serious?" She shook her head. As happy as she was to see him, they had some serious talking to do.

He said nothing for a moment, then looked around. "So this is where you work. You know, I've always wanted to see you in your work environment. Very nice."

She followed his gaze. She had just barely managed to clean up and put things away. "Thank you. I love it here."

"Bet you have a lot of clients."

"Fair amount. Thanks for recommending our service to Kyle."

"Don't thank me. He asked for the best I knew of, and I told him."

"That's very flattering."

Mark looked so handsome in a tuxedo. He'd undone his tie, and it hung loose around his neck. Nikki felt her mouth lift in a smile. It seemed as if that casual way of loosening his tie was the most recognizable habit he had. How she'd missed him!

"Well, how about it?" he said.

"How about what?"

"Coming to the reception. I can wait while you change."

"Looks like you have it all figured out." Nikki took off her apron and hung it on the hook.

"Only as far as you're concerned," Mark said with a smile. "But you'd have to agree first, of course."

Maybe this was the opportunity she'd needed to talk about why they'd split under a cloud of misunderstandings as employer and employee. "All right," Nikki said, relenting. "I'll go to the reception. By the way, how was the cake?"

"Superb. Looked like the guests couldn't get enough of it. They asked for the chef, but your assistant said she wasn't the one they should thank, that it was you." A look of amusement crossed his face. "You should have been there to take the compliments."

"It's the cake, not the chef, that's on display," Nikki said.

"For me it was the chef." He moved closer. The manly aroma of aftershave overpowered her, almost causing her to lose her resolve to keep her head. She remembered how nice he could be, and how much he'd been in her thoughts.

"Come with me to the reception, Nikki."

"I have to think about it." She took a step away from him.

He held up his hands in a gesture of surrender. "Don't worry, I won't bite. Tell you what—you go and get changed. I have a couple of things to do, so I'll pick you up after that. What's your address?"

Nikki used the action of closing up her business to give herself some time. What harm would come out of going to the wedding reception dance with Mark? She shut off the computer and put away the wax paper and white packing boxes—yet, while doing all this, she couldn't forget Mark's presence behind her, a meteor of energy that had so suddenly zapped her, and rendered her a little confused. She wanted to go, and yet she didn't, at least not until several things had been cleared up in her mind.

"We didn't part under the best of circumstances, remember?" she said.

"All the more reason you should come along. Maybe you'll listen to my side of it."

"All right. I have to go to my apartment first. You can meet me there, here's the address." Nikki wrote down her address on a slip of paper and handed it to him.

He glanced down and said, "See you later." Then he strode out of the building.

Twenty minutes later, he was standing at the door of her apartment.

"Please come in," Nikki said, stepping aside for him to

enter. "I'm not quite ready, but it'll only take me a minute."

Mark glanced around, an expression of curiosity and interest written large on his handsome face. The neat living room furniture, the vases of flowers which Nikki made sure she got from the florist round the corner, the shelves full of books on catering, all seemed to beckon to Mark.

"It's got your special stamp on it," he said finally. "I mean your apartment."

"I'll take that as a compliment."

"It's meant as one." He looked at pictures of her parents and of herself as a child with the dogs she used to have at home, savoring every detail.

"If you'll excuse me, I'll go get ready," Nikki said. "Please make yourself comfortable. There are some soft drinks in the refrigerator."

Nikki took a quick shower and wrapped a robe around her. She blew out a heaving breath. What a day! Mark shows up just when she was closing for the day and asks her to be his date at the wedding reception dance. When was the last time she'd had a date with Mark—or the last time she'd had a date?

She could drop the cool, ice-maiden act now that she was in her own room. Now she tingled all over. Mark sat in the living room waiting for her to get ready. How did that happen? Nikki would have liked to know, but that would be like looking the proverbial gift-horse in the mouth.

She opened the closet door and rifled through the dresses until she came to a short turquoise silk number and laid it on the bed. It took her only a few moments to get into her dress, brush her hair into place and put on some light lipstick and blush.

Nikki's heart raced as she opened the door and walked into the living room. Mark's back was turned to her as he stood looking at some photos on the entertainment console. He turned around sharply when she approached.

"Whoa!" He sucked in his breath and stared. "You're absolutely beautiful."

"Thank you." She smiled. She'd never seen him stunned like this before, so completely at a loss for words, and she couldn't help feeling just a little bit flattered.

"I'm just the guy who's escorting Nikki Slater to the dance," Mark said. "You look like a million dollars."

"Nice of you to say so," Nikki said, putting away the glass he had been drinking water from. She then grabbed a warm jacket. "Ready?"

"Yes, Ma'am." He held open the door for her and they walked to the parking area in the back of the building. He guided her into the car, got into the driver's seat, and started the engine.

"I was hoping you'd agree to go." Mark drove out of the parking lot, his hand resting lightly on the steering wheel.

"Why?"

"To clear up a few things."

Nikki studied his profile–the high forehead, the finely sculpted nose, and strong jaw. He could be a movie star and put the best of them to shame. She let out an unconscious sigh.

"What was *that* for?" Mark turned to her for a moment, and then back to the road.

"We do have things to clear up," Nikki said. "I was upset at your insinuations that I had ulterior motives for working for you."

"I was surprised at finding my housekeeper was from the rich Slater family. Can you blame me?" Mark shook his head. "Normally it wouldn't matter who's rich and who's not, but I jumped to the first conclusion that popped into my mind."

"I didn't get a chance to tell you about myself." Such a difference from the time Mark confronted her and they went head to head like two combatants. How sick at heart she'd been then! "You weren't in the best listening mood."

Mark swung into a long driveway lit up with a row of tall lights. Although the parking lot was full, there was an empty spot with a signed marked "Reserved" and he parked there.

"Royal treatment, huh?" Nikki said with a chuckle.

"Kyle insisted, so I could come and go as I liked." Mark grinned. "Well, here we are."

They entered the reception hall. The floor had been cleared of tables and chairs and the hall transformed into a dreamland of seductive ambience. The music was playing and its inviting tones drifted out to meet them.

Mark plucked a long-stemmed red rose from a bouquet near the entrance and handed it to Nikki. Red, for love? Surprised, she took the flower and looked into his eyes trying to discern what he was thinking.

"This is where you throw all your inhibitions out the window," Mark said, leading Nikki to the floor. "May I have this dance?"

Nikki lifted the flower to her nose and breathed in the scent. "I thought you'd never ask." No reason not to toss in a few polite amenities as long as they were play-acting. Were they? Nikki didn't think she was, and Mark seemed like he meant it when he said the things he did moments ago.

Mark wrapped his arms around her. She tingled to his touch, yet didn't want to give herself away by responding with yearning. No, she wanted to see where they were headed first.

"Tell me," Nikki said. "Did you really think I was another Marnie? Out to harness you?"

Mark laughed. "Actually, yes. Then when I saw the way

185

she behaved toward you at her barbecue and how you didn't respond in like manner, I knew you were of different material. But then I ran into you and your mother talking."

"And you thought we were dreaming up a scheme," Nikki finished. "Mother had it in her mind, but she and I are very different. That's why I wanted to make it on my own. Don't get me wrong, I love my parents, but I felt stifled in their way of life." Nikki felt his arm tighten around her gently.

"You're pretty special. I knew it right from the beginning, I just couldn't figure you out from time to time, that's all," Mark said. "I know what it is to not be able to get close to a parent, much as I admire and love Dad." A somber expression flitted across his face for a second, then it was gone.

Nikki liked to think maybe she helped to alleviate it. A new feeling crept over her. She'd like to take care of him, face him across the breakfast table each morning, make dinner for him at night, have his children. She looked away—at the band, the flowers decorating the panels on the walls—anywhere but at Mark.

Her gaze rested on Ellen standing near the edge of the crowd, watching them. A sparkle lit her face and she gave Nikki a thumbs-up sign. Nikki gasped in surprise.

"What is it?" Mark asked.

"Ellen's watching us. You don't think...?"

"That she'd like to see us as a couple? Yes, I do. And since I've decided to give her the condo, she'll be around quite often."

"You're still going to do that?" Nikki asked, trying to keep her disappointment at bay.

"Well, Gran is going to live in her own house, but she'll still have the condo for when she comes into town," Mark said.

Nikki looked up at him quickly. "I'm so glad."

"I knew you'd be," Mark said. "Now I have something to ask you."

"Ask me?"

"Will you marry me? Can you forget I've been a pig-headed dunce?"

It was true about flowers blooming when they weren't even there and a thousand violins playing and bells ringing, because that's just what she thought she heard. "I'd like that very much."

"Wait right here," Mark said, and strode off toward the band and said something to them. Soon, they started playing "*My Girl*."

Mark returned, took Nikki in his arms, and whirled her smoothly around the floor. "This one's for you. You're my girl and I love you." He leaned his cheek against her head. "Tomorrow we'll have to tell Gran the good news."

"Wonderful idea," Nikki said. "Don't forget your dad."

"I hadn't. I feel so great that I don't even mind Marnie as a relative. I just wish she was good for Dad, though."

"Maybe things will get better." Nikki smiled up at him.

"I'm wishing everyone could have the luck I just found," Mark said, holding her tighter.

"I know someone who's going to be very happy with our news," Nikki said.

"Who?"

"My mother."

They both chuckled. "She means well, just like parents always do," Mark said.

"I know. It just took me a while to find out." And Nikki snuggled closer, feeling warm and loved as she had never been before.

Meet the author:

Rekha Ambardar published over fifty mystery, mainstream and literary short stories in print magazines, including Eureka Literary Magazine, Futures, Writer's Journal, The Writing Class, and in electronic magazines such as Twilight Times, Nefarious, Zuzu's Petals Quarterly, Star of Hope Anthology (Inspirational), Writers Hood, Electronic Writers' Journal, and poems in poetry anthologies. She has published articles in ByLine, Writer's Journal, Simple Joy, The Writer's Life, The National Association of Women Writers' Guide Weekly, St. Louis Writers' Guide Weekly, The Indian Express, and book reviews in the Ann Arbor News.

She teaches business communication and marketing at the International School of Business at Finlandia University, Hancock, Michigan. Her short contemporary romance novel, HIS HARBOR GIRL is available from Whiskey Creek Press.

Visit Rekha at

http://rekha.mmebj.com/

.

Coming
Fall 2005
From Echelon Press

Heart's Desire

By

Deborah Grace-Staley

Book Three

In the

Angel Ridge Series

~*~

"Dispatch. Do you have an emergency?"

"Well, not unless you call some missing underwear an emergency."

The woman's low-pitched warm laugher flowed through the line, caressing Grady Wallace's ear and firing his blood.

He cleared his throat and checked the Caller ID. Heart's Desire. Owner and Proprietor, one very single, very hot, Candi Heart. "What can I help you with, Candi?"

"That you, Sheriff? Since when did you start answering the phone over there?"

"Today's Clara's birthday, so I gave her the day off."

"Oh, that's right. Frank called and made a pedicure appointment for her. Ordered up a dozen roses, too. Nice to see folks that have been together that long still in love."

Grady frowned. The town's typically upbeat hair stylist sounded almost wistful. "What's going on over there, Candi?"

"Oh, sorry Grady. I don't mean to ramble. It's just, someone broke in here–"

"A break in?" Grady's instincts torpedoed to full alert. "When?"

"Well, I guess it was sometime overnight–"

"Listen close, Candi. Don't move and keep quiet. I'll be right over."

"Oh, no! You don't have to–"

Grady hung the phone up on her protests and called out to his deputy, "Catch the phone, Woody. I got something I need to check out."

"Sure thing, Grady. Call if you need back-up."

"Yeah," Grady said, but he was already sprinting up the stairs that led out the back of the jail and up the walkway that wound around to the front of the courthouse. By the time he hit the town's sidewalk, he was sprinting. A cool autumn morning breeze stung his arms, but he barely noticed.

A bell tinkled as he passed through the entrance of Heart's Desire. He pulled the gun from his shoulder holster and clicked the safety off. Candi appeared from the back of the salon, nearly giving him a heart attack.

"Jeez oh Pete, Grady!" Candi held out a hand between them. "Put that thing away."

He missed a step–and forgot to breathe. He swept her with a quick, assessing glance. Her Asian heritage gave her an exotic look that he'd always found incredibly appealing. Her fashion sense was just plain provocative. Today she wore a brief, black skirt that barely covered the essentials. Add to that a form-fitting sweater with barely buttoned Oxford shirt hanging below it. He caught a flash of silver in her belly button as she moved toward him. With her long, dark hair up in dog-ears, it all combined to give him the hottest schoolgirl fantasy he'd ever experienced.

He shook his head. *Come on, Grady. Get hold of yourself! You got a crime to investigate.* He grasped Candi by the arm and pulled her behind him. "I thought I told you to stay put," he said gruffly.

"Hey, careful with the merchandise, big guy."

He turned and pinned her with a "no arguments" kind of look. "Stay here."

He proceeded into the salon, scanning every inch to make sure the intruder hadn't stuck around after breaking in. He dodged into the Naughty Room. A display case had been broken into. Shattered glass littered the floor. The heavy scent of perfume hung in the air. An exotic scent that did strange things to him. It brought to mind long, hot summer nights–

He backed out of the room and went across the hall to the Nice Salon. It appeared untouched.

The beauty salon in the back also seemed undisturbed. A window stood open on the back wall. He took a moment to compose himself before he rejoined Candi in the front. Had it been so long since he'd had a call he'd forgotten how to act professionally?

He raked a hand through his hair. Sure, he'd seen Candi around since she'd opened her controversial business in town, but he kept his distance. Her brand of blatant sexuality and the strong way he typically reacted to her, frankly threw him off-balance. A man in his position couldn't afford that kind of distraction.

He also knew enough about her family to know that he was a conventional kind of guy, and nothing about Candi and her family–if you could call it that–was conventional. He dragged in a deep breath and returned to the front.

Candi smiled as a tingle of awareness swept through her body. She crossed her arms as the sheriff moved toward the back, alert to any movement, gun drawn. She shrugged. Might as was well enjoy the view. Getting ripped-off was a real drag, but having Angel Ridge's finest in her establishment was certainly no hardship. To say he wore his uniform well would be an understatement.

Tall and muscular, his khaki slacks were pressed to within an inch of their life, as was his matching shirt. At odds was that the fact that his usually short, neat hairstyle was in need of a trim. She chewed on her lower lip. She could take care of that. How she'd love to sink her hands into those thick, brownish-red tresses.

She leaned against the glass-enclosed case in the front. He seriously had the widest shoulders she'd ever seen. She tipped her head to the side as he checked out the boutiques and followed the long hallway back to the salon. He stood in the entry to the salon longer than she would have expected. No matter. It gave her more time to look. A thick brown belt emphasized his narrow waist and the way his pants hugged a very fine–

"All clear."

He returned to the front of the shop where she had fresh flowers and candies, securing his handgun to its holster as long-legged strides brought him closer.

She smiled. "Could have told you we were alone if you would have let me talk."

"Better safe than sorry. I've seen cases where the owner thought the thief had left, and he was still lurking in the store, waiting to–" He cut off abruptly, then pulled a notepad out of a shirt pocket.

Candi's gaze lingered a bit longer than necessary at the open collar of his shirt. He had a nice, muscular chest, too....

Grady cleared his throat. "So, what happened, Candi? You missin' some merchandise?"

She took her time pulling her eyes up to meet his steady hazel gaze. He was looking at her expectantly. Well, if he was waiting for an apology, he'd have a long wait. She wasn't about to apologize for admiring a good-looking man. Besides, he'd had a pretty good look at her earlier. So, she gave him a slow smile. "Follow me."

She put a little more swing in her walk than necessary. A girl had to work it when she got the opportunity, after all. A quick glance back at him as she passed through the purple beaded curtain of the Naughty Boutique confirmed that the effort had not been wasted.

So, the Sheriff liked what he saw… She filed that tidbit away for future use. She'd lived in Angel Ridge all her life, but not having attended public school with everyone else, or church for that matter, her contact with the people in town had been limited to the time she'd spent behind the bar at her dad's pool hall. When Grady had come in, he'd either been on duty or with friends. Always polite, but keeping his distance.

The scent of wild, exotic orchids hung heavy in the room from where the burglar had knocked over a display of her signature perfumes. She'd been trying to sweep the mess up when Grady arrived.

"Sorry about the perfume. Who ever ripped me off took out about four hundred dollars worth of perfumes I'd made and put in antique atomizers while he was stumbling around in here looking for women's underwear."

She retrieved the dustpan and broom and stooped to continue cleaning up the glass.

"Here, let me do that."

His fingers brushed hers as he took the pan and handheld broom from her. Their gazes locked in a charged moment that stole her breath. The man had incredible eyes. Earlier, they'd been a green-gold hazel mix. Now they were a deep, intense sea green. She was having hot fantasies about diving in.

"I'm sorry you have to deal with this, Candi. Don't worry, I'll track the perp down."

"Thanks." She stood while he swept up the rest of the glass and tried to compose herself. Earlier, she'd engaged in a little good-natured flirting with the sheriff, but a second ago, when their eyes had met, well, she felt he'd looked into her eyes and reached right down to her soul. She wasn't sure if she liked the feeling or if she wanted to explore it further.

He stood and she smoothed a hand over her skirt. "Here, let me dump that." He handed her the pan, and she used the few seconds it took to dispose of the glass in the wastebasket to regain her frayed composure.

"So, why don't you give me a rundown on what was taken?"

"Oh, sure." She moved over to the display case and he followed. "*Um*, three, no, four pairs of edible thongs…and two bottles of amaretto massage oil." She tapped a finger against her lower lip and tried to focus on something other than the sexy as sin sheriff standing next to her.

He coughed, then cleared his throat. "Excuse me."

"Can it get you some water?" She waved a hand in front of her face. "That perfume's pretty thick. Hope you're not allergic."

"No. I'm good, thanks." He adjusted the walkie-talkie at his hip. "Did you say, edible thongs?"

"Yeah. Four pairs."

He frowned, then made a note and added, "And massage oil? Two bottles?"

She leaned toward him to look at what he had written. Pointing to the paper she said, "Amaretto massage oil. You know, it's flavored 'cause after the massage, you lick–"

"Got it. Amaretto. Anything else?"

Well, well. The town's finest was blushing like a schoolboy. "Let's see… Whoever it was, busted the display case open to get at the stuff. I probably oughta inventory the stock to see if any of that's missing. There's no telling just at a glance."

"Okay. When you get that done, let me know and I'll add it to the report." Walking over to the perimeter of the room, he asked, "You think they got in through that window in the back?"

Following him, she said, "Probably."

"You left a window open?"

Embrace the Passion with an
Echelon Embrace

Ain't Love Grand
ISBN 1-59080-298-5

Dana Taylor
$10.99

Against the Rules
ISBN 1-59080-310-8

Natalie Damschroder
$14.49

Zorroc
ISBN 1-59080-318-3

Lil Gibson
$13.99

A Brush With Love
ISBN 1-59080-266-7

Jo Barrett
$11.99

House of Cards
ISBN 1-59080-187-3

Blair Wing
$10.99

Just Kiss Me
ISBN 1-59080-174-1

Sarah Storme
$13.49

Dark Shines My Love
ISBN 1-59080-252-7

Alexis Hart
$10.99

Caribbean Charade
ISBN 1-59080-209-8

Louise Perry
$11.99

Operation: Stiletto
ISBN 1-59080-392-2

T.A. Ridgell
$14.49

Raphaela's Gift
ISBN 1-59080-277-2

Sydney Laine Allan
$13.99

To order visit
www.echelonpress.com
Or visit your local
Retail bookseller

Printed in the United States
70568LV00001B/13-18